WANDERING ANGUS

by the same author

novels

Natana
Kintalloch
The Hawthorn Hedge
Langwheeple

short stories
Teresa's Decision

translation
Weir de Hermiston i altres relats
(R. L. Stevenson's *Weir of Hermiston* in Catalan)

Wandering Angus

A Kintalloch Novel

Mercedes Clarasó

BLACK ACE BOOKS

First published in 1998 by Black Ace Books
PO Box 6557, Forfar, DD8 2YS, Scotland

© Mercedes Clarasó 1998

Typeset in Scotland by Black Ace Editorial

Printed in Great Britain by Redwood Books
Kennet Way, Trowbridge, BA14 6RN

A CIP catalogue record for this book
is available from the British Library

ISBN   1–872988–07–5

The publishers gratefully acknowledge
subsidy from the Scottish Arts Council
towards the production of this first edition

We also thank A.P. Watt Ltd on behalf of Michael Yeats
for permission to include 'The Song of Wandering Aengus'
taken from *The Collected Poems of W.B. Yeats*

THE SONG OF WANDERING AENGUS

I WENT out to the hazel wood,
Because a fire was in my head,
And cut and peeled a hazel wand,
And hooked a berry to a thread;
And when white moths were on the wing,
And moth-like stars were flickering out,
I dropped the berry in a stream
And caught a little silver trout.

When I had laid it on the floor
I went to blow the fire aflame,
But something rustled on the floor,
And some one called me by my name;
It had become a glimmering girl
With apple blossom in her hair
Who called me by my name and ran
And faded through the brightening air.

Though I am old with wandering
Through hollow lands and hilly lands,
I will find out where she has gone,
And kiss her lips and take her hands;
And walk among long dappled grass,
And pluck till time and times are done
The silver apples of the moon,
The golden apples of the sun.

W.B. Yeats, 1899

1

Gil Cardona and his mule were slowly climbing up the rocky track from the village. They had decided to take it easy. It had been a long day, and they still had more than two miles to climb before reaching the *masia* on the little plateau so improbably scooped out of the side of the mountain. They had stopped for a rest when they heard the sound of a motor on the road high above them. More troops on their way to the Ebro front, thought Gil. Then he heard the planes and saw them swooping down towards the road. He knew he would hear the machine-gun fire in a moment, and it came as expected. He watched as the planes flew away, circled and came back. After the second round of firing the planes flew off again in the direction from which they had come.

'*Apa, noi,*' he said to the mule and gave it an encouraging whack on the rear. A few minutes later he heard the engine of the truck starting up again. Well, he thought, they can't all have been killed. I wonder how many corpses I'll find.

When they came to the road, instead of crossing it and following the upward track in the usual way, Gil took the bridle and led the mule along the road. The animal responded with alacrity, as if it couldn't believe its luck. To be invited to walk along the smooth, nearly level road was a piece of good fortune that seldom came its way.

Gil had a good idea of what part of the road the attack must have taken place on, and soon found what he was looking for – eight or nine bodies scattered on both sides of the road. He knew exactly what to do. Not that he had ever been in this situation before. But the countryside was full of tales of bodies left unburied after a similar attack. And the thing to do, as he had learned, was to go through all the pockets, taking any money or other valuables that were to be had. At first the idea had shocked him, but the arguments had been convincing. After all, the money was of no use whatever to the original owners. And there was no chance that it would ever find its way to the families of the victims. We're all poor, the argument ran, we all need the money. Only a fool would refuse to take it.

Gil stood still for a while, looking abstractedly at the dead men and thinking about how the day's business had gone, in an attempt to assess his right to any wealth that was to be had in the pockets of the victims. He'd got quite a good price for the two kids, it was true; but then, he'd had to pay so much more for all his provisions. Food was getting scarcer every day, and prices were rising. The oil, for instance, had cost more than double what he'd had to pay last month. And the flour! The white stuff was so dear that he'd decided against buying any, and had got some ugly, coarse, yellowish stuff instead. Marta wouldn't be pleased. As for the fodder for the animals, it was so dear he just didn't know what to do. With winter about to come on he couldn't afford not to get in his supplies. And yet the price was outrageous. He had hesitated for a while, then decided he'd better get it. It would probably be even dearer by his next visit in a week's time.

Altogether, he decided, he couldn't afford to be squeamish

about this. He knelt down heavily beside the nearest corpse. Foreigners, he thought, as he looked at the fair skin and golden hair. Must be those Englishmen from the International Brigade. Poor young devils, why did they have to come and get mixed up in this?

Finding the money was an unpleasant business. Most of the victims had bled freely, and he soon had blood on both his hands. But he persevered, and found both silver and notes. It was a wonderful windfall. Kneeling beside the last victim he drew a passport out of the breast pocket, and opened it to see if there were any notes in it, for that seemed to be where most of them carried their paper money. He drew out a few one hundred peseta notes, and as he did so a little piece of paper fell out and was immediately blown away by a gust of wind. Gil made no effort to retrieve it. After all, what was the point? It now meant nothing to anybody. He had been careful to put all the passports back where he found them. If anyone came for the corpses it would be a means of identification.

As he slipped this last passport into its corresponding pocket he started back suddenly. He could have sworn that the corpse had given something like a sigh. He examined him more thoroughly and came to the conclusion that the man was breathing.

'*Verge santissima!*' he exclaimed, and crossed himself. Like many Spaniards, he managed to combine a healthy anticlericalism with a superstitious fear that the priests might be right after all.

What was he to do now? The first practical step that occurred to him was to put the money back into the passport. He certainly wasn't going to steal from a living man.

He stood up and tried to think of the best thing to do. The easiest thing would be to leave the poor fellow alone. He had evidently been shot in the stomach, the legs, and one shoulder. It was almost certain that he would die. But meanwhile he was still alive, and his only hope of salvation lay in appropriate action on his, Gil's, part. He could put him on the mule and take him back down to the village. But that would take even longer than climbing back up to the *masia*. And anyway, there was no doctor in the village. Marta could probably look after him as well as anyone down there. The best thing would be to load him on to the mule and take him home.

Carefully he put all the rest of the money into his pocket, reflecting that he now had more ready money in his possession than he normally had in the course of several years. Then he unloaded the mule. He would have to come back for the stuff later on. He took care to hide his provisions as best he could behind the rocks and bushes, just in case anyone came along.

Then came the difficult bit. The stranger was taller than Gil, and well built. It wasn't easy to lift him on to the mule, especially since he was so badly injured and so had to be handled with great care. He wasn't happy about the injured man's position on the animal, with his head and shoulders hanging over one side, and his legs dangling over the other, but that was all he could do.

As he trudged along beside the mule he wondered how he would break the news to Marta, and whether she would be dismayed at the prospect of having such a sick man to look after, or thrilled to see how much money they had suddenly acquired. He decided she'd better not see the injured man till he'd explained the situation, and so he left the mule outside instead of bringing it into the hall, as was the usual practice.

'Marta!' he called, as he made his way to the kitchen. Marta appeared in the doorway and let out a piercing scream as soon as she saw him.

'My God, what's happened to you?'

It was only then that he realized that he'd forgotten to do anything about the blood on his hands and clothes.

After his explanation things weren't much better.

'You should have taken him to the village,' she said. 'If the priest finds out we've got one of those foreign Reds here we'll be in trouble, I can tell you.'

Gil bowed his head. He hadn't thought of that.

'Well,' he said after a moment's thought, 'he's here and we've got to look after him. Just make sure you don't tell a soul. Come and help me get him in.'

Marta went out grudgingly, but melted when she saw the stranger's face.

'*Sembla un Sant Crist*,' she said. And indeed Angus, with his fair hair and beard, his closed eyes and the expression of suffering on his face looked like a representation of the crucified Christ. Marta forgot all about her fears in her eagerness to get the injured man into the house as gently as possible.

'We'll put him in Quimeta's bed,' she said. 'She can sleep in the loft. She won't mind.'

As she bustled about, getting water and clean cloths to bathe the wounds, Gil explained about the money.

'Did you take any from him?' she asked.

'Yes . . . now, don't start making a fuss. I thought he was dead. I put it back as soon as I saw he was alive.'

Marta cut short her protest and asked Gil how much money he'd got.

'Hundreds of pesetas. Far, far more than we've ever had all at once.'

2

For weeks Angus lay in a semi-conscious state, aware of nothing but pain and confusion. He had no idea of where he was, or of who he was. At first he didn't even have any knowledge of separate identity. Gradually awareness increased, and he began to notice a woman's face bent over him, talking quietly in a language he couldn't make out. The woman was middle-aged, with a pale, careworn face and greying hair.

Sometimes there was another figure with her. She too spoke softly, and when she came near enough he was able to see a face of the most perfect beauty. It was like a very young and human embodiment of the Virgin Mary. For a long time he took this to be a trick of his feverish condition. In the end he came to accept her reality, and kept his eyes on her, delighting in her beauty. She looked very young, perhaps twelve or thirteen years old – a child, really. And yet there was a stillness and repose about her that seemed to belong more to a grown woman.

After his wounds had healed and his strength come back he was left with the conviction that the presence of this exquisite being had played an important part in his recovery. Merely looking at her brought a sense of peace and fulfilment.

As his mental faculties returned he began to take stock of his surroundings. He was in a very small room with a low ceiling. The walls were whitewashed, the beams painted black. There was one tiny window, through which, as he lay in bed, he could see nothing but sky. There were one or two pieces of primitive-looking furniture against the walls. That was all. He knew from the sound of the steps approaching and retreating that he must be upstairs. Also, he was sometimes aware of voices coming from somewhere below. Occasionally a man came and looked at him, then went away again, shaking his head. He looked about the same age as the woman, and was dressed in the usual corduroy of the Catalan peasant. His face was lined like the woman's, as if he too had had a hard life.

Slowly Angus's memory began to come back to him. Scenes from his past life seemed to float about him, disconnected and confusing. Gradually he was able to piece them all together into a coherent, chronological whole. It all ended with Bob's death. He remembered laying his friend's head gently on the ground and standing up to look for Dick. And then the planes had come again.

His recovery was extremely slow. He had lost so much blood that he was too weak to cope adequately with the healing process, and one of the leg wounds became infected. He suspected later that, had there been any medical attention available, he would almost certainly have suffered an amputation.

As it was, the treatment consisted of a change of bandages twice a day, and tisanes to drink made from different herbs. The recipe varied according to the state that Marta considered the patient to be in — thyme and rosemary to act as a tonic, aniseed and basil to aid digestion, fennel and camomile to soothe.

It was weeks before any form of verbal communication took place, and it was a slow and difficult business at first. Angus, with his love of languages, had learned a certain amount of Spanish in France, and had practised it a little since his arrival in Spain. His Spanish was by no means correct, but it was good enough to get by. Here, however, in this mountain retreat, his hosts spoke virtually nothing but Catalan. They had, of course, been taught Castilian Spanish at school – but then, they had spent very little time at school, and had hardly ever used the language since. After a while Angus discovered that he got on just as well speaking French to them, mingled with the few words of Catalan that he had picked up since his arrival on Catalan soil.

In this slow and painful manner he managed eventually to piece together some of the particulars that he was most anxious to know – how he had got there, where he was, who lived in the house. Most of all he wanted to find out more about the beautiful girl. He discovered that she was called Quimeta and that she was their only surviving daughter. When he asked about her age he was shocked to learn that she was twenty-two years old. He couldn't believe it. She looked ten years younger; and besides, he had seen her playing with an ancient and filthy wooden doll.

Marta saw the shocked expression on his face and shook her head sadly. 'She'll always be a child,' she said. 'Up here,' and she pointed to her forehead, 'she's only about six years old.'

Angus could find no adequate words to express his sympathy. All he could do was murmur, '*Triste, très triste.*'

'*Sí, molt trist, molt trist.*' The woman sighed, then drew herself up resolutely. 'It's the cross we have to bear. The cross Our Lord has sent us. We all have our cross to bear.

You too.' And she held out her hands above the bed in a gesture that seemed to take in all his wounds.

Quimeta spent a lot of time in the room, looking with rapt eyes at the heaven-sent stranger. There were moments when she was convinced that he was Jesus in person, and she would stand near the door, gazing at him in adoration.

The discovery of her age and her mental condition had been a terrible blow to Angus. In the first place, he was intensely distressed on her parents' account, and wondered how they could accept the situation with so little bitterness. Later on, as communication improved, he was to learn that having a subnormal child was not such an unusual thing in these rural areas. Down in the village there were half a dozen, and it was taken for granted that any moderately large family was likely to produce at least one example of the feeble-minded or misshapen. He discovered that he was in the midst of an extremely isolated community, and that in-breeding was only too common.

Their little farm was the most far-flung of them all, and had virtually no visitors of any kind, which was why it was possible to keep him there in complete secrecy. But, for many miles around, the other farms were nearly as isolated, and the only connexion with the rest of the world that their inhabitants enjoyed was through their periodic visits to the little village far below. In winter, he learned – and winter had set in with a vengeance by that time – it was sometimes impossible to get down to the village for weeks on end.

'But what do you do if you run short of supplies?'

Marta looked up and gave him a queer little smile. 'We do without,' she said.

Pondering over that smile, Angus decided that it had been made up of amusement and pride. Pride in their own strength and endurance, amusement at the stranger who could not envisage doing without the things he always took for granted.

His other reason for feeling distress over Quimeta's condition was more personal. During the worst weeks of his illness the sight of Quimeta's dark, compassionate eyes on him had brought him so much comfort that he had indulged in one fantasy after another about the girl. They all ended up the same way. When he was better, when she was old enough, he would come back and claim her as his bride.

Since Nancy's death he had had no stable relationship with any woman. He had come to the conclusion that he simply wasn't capable of living harmoniously with anyone for long. But with this tender and trusting creature it would be different. After the war was over they would find some tiny, humble farm like this, and settle down to a lifetime of rustic content. The frustrated longing for life at Kintalloch, the sense of family, would be transferred to the mountains of Catalonia. The dream was sweet, none the less sweet for its impracticality; he was in no state to think of the harsh realities of the situation.

After the discovery of Quimeta's retarded state he reacted violently against her, and found it very hard to support her presence with equanimity. The memory of his shattered dreams added to his discomfiture, and he felt intensely uncomfortable when she was near. It was almost as if she had unwittingly played a trick on him. He realized, naturally, that the mistake would never have taken place had it not been for the weakened and confused state in which he had first become aware of her presence, and for the extreme difficulty in communication which he had experienced till some sort of a lingua franca had been set up between him and the parents.

As his physical state gradually improved he became able to

view the matter in a less tragic light. The dream of marriage to Quimeta must go, of course. But he was now able to see that it had been nothing but a foolish fancy anyway. The essence of the girl, and of what she had meant to him, remained unchanged. She had lost none of her beauty or her gentleness or her compassion. Her smile was just as radiant, her voice as soft as when he first heard her murmuring her cryptic syllables or singing her doll to sleep. At no time had he admired her for her intellectual gifts. This aspect simply hadn't come into their relationship. The look in her eyes, the serene oval of her face framed in the dark cloud of her hair; these were the things that had worked on him, and they remained unchanged.

Once again he began to feel that there was some sort of non-verbal communication between them. He remembered what Bob had said to him about children being more intuitive than adults. Perhaps Quimeta, in her wholly non-rational way, was able to relate to him more fully than her more articulate parents. If language was indeed given to man in order to enable him to conceal his thoughts, Quimeta had no such subterfuge at her disposal. Her verbal communication was on the most elementary level only. But her eyes spoke for her, and they spoke the truth.

3

As the state of his injured guest's health improved, Gil spent more time with him, and after a while they were able to communicate reasonably well. Angus's chief concern was to try and find out anything he could about Dick. He did his best to describe him, and discovered that there was really nothing particularly distinctive about his friend's appearance to help in the description. There was nothing unusual about his features and colouring; and it was unlikely that the eager, open, happy expression had survived death. They came to the conclusion that there was no way in which Gil could say definitely whether he had been among the dead left lying when the truck had continued its journey.

It was now many weeks since the incident, and even if Angus had been able to get about, a visit to the scene of the attack would have achieved nothing. Gil had told him that by the time he went down to the village the following week the corpses had been removed. All Angus could do was hope that Dick had been able to get away alive. He resolved that, as soon as he could get back to England, the first thing he would do would be to contact Dick's parents. He remembered the name of the small village in Essex where they lived, so there should be no problem in finding them.

He had often thought of his promise to go and see Bob's parents in the event of their son's death. Just as well Bob had written down the address. To find a family called Gray in a place the size of Bradford would be a difficult matter without the correct address.

Quimeta was standing by the door, watching him as usual. He signed to her to bring over his jacket, which, sponged clean and mended, was hanging over the back of the chair. The girl brought it over, and Angus began feeling for the passport in the breast pocket. His right shoulder had been shattered by one of the bullets, and he could not use this arm at all. The shoulder had been allowed to set by itself, and he wondered whether he would ever be able to use the arm again. Meanwhile, he must learn to do everything with his left hand.

He found the passport, opened it, and discovered rather more money in it than he was expecting. After counting the hundred peseta notes he became even more puzzled.

He knew for a certainty that he had not had more than two on him – he remembered discussing with Bob how much money each was carrying as they set off in the truck. And now there were four in his passport. He simply couldn't account for it. As for the slip of paper with the address, it had disappeared. He searched long and wearily in every pocket, but with no result. How on earth was he going to get in touch with Bob's parents now?

He lay back exhausted, and decided he would have to think up some method later on, when his mind was clearer. Besides, as long as he was in this remote farm perched on the side of a Catalan mountain, there was no immediate hurry. It might be months yet before he could leave.

Meanwhile the puzzle about the money remained. The next time Marta appeared he decided to ask her. He had difficulty in formulating his question. When at last she understood that he was talking about the money in his pocket she blushed crimson and left the room, looking very agitated. Angus felt rather agitated too, for he realized that she probably thought he was accusing them of having taken some, and cursed himself for his insensitivity. Better to be left with the mystery unexplained than to upset these good people with what they might consider an accusation. And even if it had been the other way round, even if he had found less money than he expected, he would never have thought of complaining. Weren't they feeding and caring for him, with no talk of any kind of reward? It was clear that they lived a very spartan existence, that their usual scarcity of supplies was exacerbated by the war, and he knew that feeding him must be an added burden on them. And yet they had said nothing. Why had he not thought of it before? He should have offered them every penny he possessed.

He could hear some earnest conversation going on downstairs, and wished that he could go down and explain that he was making no accusations. After a while Gil came up, looking rather embarrassed. He understood there was some problem about the money? Angus managed to explain that his problem was that he'd got too much.

To his surprise, this information made Gil look even more uncomfortable. He shuffled from one foot to the other, and finally managed to explain about how he had taken the money, including what he had found in Angus's passport, and put this back when he saw Angus was still alive. As he hadn't counted the exact amount he must have put back more than he had taken out. They had a slightly awkward laugh about it, and then Angus took two of the notes and held them out to Gil. 'They're not mine,' he said.

Gil refused to take them, on the grounds that they weren't

his either. Angus pointed out that he must take them, if only to pay for the expenses incurred in looking after him. Gil pointed out that Angus would need all the money he could get hold of when he left. In the end they sent for Marta, and it was agreed that the money should be put aside for use by whoever needed it first.

That matter settled, Angus asked about the slip of paper with Bob's address. Gil had forgotten all about it, but remembered now, and had to confess that it had blown away. He looked apologetic. 'I didn't think you'd need it.'

Angus laughed. 'Of course not. You thought I was dead.'

'I'm sorry. I could have caught it if I'd known. And by the time I realized you were alive, I had other things to think of.'

Angus smiled reassuringly. 'You had quite a different problem on your hands by then, hadn't you?' He was just thankful that the possible misunderstanding about the money had been cleared up. And he would find some way or other of getting in touch with Bob's parents.

Marta had been very upset by what she had taken to be an accusation on Angus's part. She had nursed him with devotion, first of all as an exercise in Christian duty, and also because that was what her husband had told her to do, and then, as she got to know him, for his own sake. The thought of any ill feeling between them hurt her deeply, and she was immensely relieved when the matter was cleared up.

When she went back downstairs to attend to her chickpea stew she was surprised to find how upset she had been. Partly by nature and partly because of the isolated life she led, she was given to introspection, and set about trying to find out why the incident had upset her so much. She had never read a book in her life, had never travelled beyond the two or three nearby villages, had only heard the radio on her rare visits to the village down below, had virtually no friends, for no-one came as far up as their farm, and she was too busy to go visiting; so, while her hands were busy her mind was free to examine her own feelings, and she had learned to know herself pretty well.

It didn't take her long to discover that her feelings for Angus were less like those of a mother for her son than she had imagined. That, surely, was a sin. She must go to church and confess it. Then she realized that she dare make no such confession to the priest, who knew the lives of his parishioners in every detail, and must know that there was no-one in her daily life about whom she could entertain such thoughts. She was a devout Catholic, and had never in her life failed to confess anything in her thoughts and behaviour that she considered a sin. Now it seemed that it was her duty to keep silent about this one.

She was sorely puzzled as to what she should do. To say anything that could possibly compromise the family or Angus would be sinful. She knew only too well that the slightest suspicion, even if aroused in the secrecy of the confessional, would send the priest right up to the farm, nosing around to see what he could find out. If he discovered that they were harbouring a Red . . .

She was driven to the conclusion that it was her duty to commit the sin of not confessing her illicit feelings for this stranger. She was confused and ashamed and afflicted, and in her distress decided that the only thing she could do was tell her troubles to the Virgin and beg her for help. There at least she knew there would be no double standards. The priest was the servant of God, and as such had to be obeyed; but he was also a hard, suspicious, acrimonious man, and as such had to be feared.

But the Virgin was all love, and would have compassion for her.

Having found this comforting solution to her dilemma, Marta was free to think again about what Angus had come to mean in her life.

4

Marta had never met, or even seen, a foreigner before Angus appeared on the scene. Even if he had proved to be a less attractive character, the effect of such closeness was bound to make a deep impression on her. Apart from the most superficial contacts, her knowledge of men was limited to her own family – at home, before her marriage, there had been her father and her brothers; since her marriage, Gil and her sons. She had not been in love with Gil when she married him. Her parents had indicated that this was a suitable match, and she had obeyed their wishes. Nor had she ever had cause to regret the decision. Gil was an upright, independent, hardworking man; rather stern, rather silent, but never harsh, never unreasonable. And if their standard of living was little above subsistence level, that was what she was used to, that was what she had been brought up to expect.

As for her sons, they had all married and left home when they were little more than boys. She was fond of them and proud of them. But they had been unable to provide her with a model of what a mature man could be. When they had left home they had seen nothing and done nothing beyond the limits of their own small circle.

And now this stranger had come, with the glamour of a

foreign world about him. Marta realized very clearly that the degree of friendship that had sprung up between them was entirely due to the special circumstances that had brought them together. Without his extreme physical helplessness, and the need for secrecy that kept him hidden away in her house, their intimacy would never have developed. Only the exceptional circumstances of war could have brought them together. And she had no illusions about the future. As soon as Angus was able to undertake the journey, he would leave. There was nothing to keep him on their barren little patch of mountainside. He would go, as her sons had gone.

The first day that Angus was able to hobble over to the window and look out, he had his first view of the surroundings in which he had spent the last months. He recognized the type of mountain landscape through which they had been driving when the truck had been attacked. Only now they were much higher than the road, and the late summer colours had changed to predominantly white and black. Rocks and rock faces stood out against the blanket of snow. Further down he could see clusters of trees so dark that they too looked black. And the sky was a pale grey, so pale that it looked hardly any darker than the white of the snow. He thought of the dislike Bob had felt for the 'bloody mountains'. In spite of his loyalty to his dead friend he couldn't help feeling uplifted by the stern grandeur of the scene. The minute world he had lived in for the last few months had suddenly expanded.

His world expanded again a few days later when he hobbled over to the door and was able to see something more of the geography of the house. He could now look into the main bedroom, where Marta and Gil slept. It was larger than his – or rather, Quimeta's – but furnished along equally austere lines. At the end of the corridor he could see the loft, and knew that this was where Quimeta now slept. He felt less guilty about being the cause of her sleeping there than he would have before coming to Spain and having to sleep rough on so many occasions. A warm loft with plenty of straw was a pretty comfortable place to be.

He could see down the stairs into the main entrance hall, which in winter acted as a stable for the mule, two cows, several goats and sundry smaller creatures. The warmth from the animals rose to the bedrooms, as did the rich odour of which he had been aware as he lay in bed. The only other room in the house was the kitchen, also on the ground floor, but on a slightly higher level. Through its open door he could see into a room with a red-tiled floor on which the flickering light of a fire was playing.

'You'll see it all when you can manage the stairs,' said Marta, with just a touch of pride. 'You'll like the kitchen. We're nice and cosy there in winter.'

By the time he was able to get downstairs spring had come, and he stood in the doorway and looked at the changed scene. The snow had gone from all but the higher slopes, and the landscape looked less austere, though still hardly welcoming.

On his weekly visits to the village Gil picked up all the information he could about the course of the war. By the time Angus was able to get up it was all but over. Barcelona had fallen and the government had fled northwards to Figueras. Hundreds of thousands of refugees had taken the road to France in their anxiety to evade Franco's advancing army. The International Brigade had been disbanded. Early in April Gil brought the news that Madrid had fallen some days before.

The war was over.

'The priests will be glad,' was Gil's comment.

Angus's position now was even worse than before. There was no longer any chance of his being able to leave the country through Republican-held territory. And for anyone suspected of having been on the losing side, the frontiers were firmly closed. If his recovery had been a little more rapid he could have joined the huge wave of refugees that the triumphant Franco troops had swept before them. But it was too late for that now.

Sitting round the fire in the kitchen, in the cold spring evenings, they spent many an hour discussing the problem. In the end they agreed that his only hope of getting out of the country was to make his way over the mountains, once he was well enough to tackle such a journey, and hope to slip into France at some unguarded spot. It was a big undertaking for a stranger who knew nothing of the rough and hostile terrain he was going to have to tackle without a guide, without even a map to help him find his way. One of the added difficulties was that he would have to keep as far away as possible from other human beings. There was no way of disguising the fact that he was a foreigner. In the circumstances he could hardly be taken for a tourist. Spain's natural xenophobia, added to the almost hysterical distrust of strangers and foreigners that came in the aftermath of the Civil War, almost guaranteed an enforced visit to the nearest Guardia Civil post if he were seen. This meant he would have to avoid all roads and keep to mountain tracks. It also meant that he would have some difficulty in getting provisions, once the stock he could carry with him was exhausted.

It was a daunting prospect.

But they all agreed that the biggest danger lay in falling into the hands of the authorities. The best, the very best, that he could hope for in that event was to be thrown into prison. They were beginning to hear something of the ferocity of the

27

retaliatory measures that were being inflicted on the defeated enemy, and felt certain that anyone with Angus's antecedents would have a very slight chance of survival.

As his strength returned Angus decided he'd better get into training. Every morning he would set off on his own, always climbing upwards and away from the village, to avoid being seen. At first he could only manage a few hundred yards. Later, as his muscles began to respond, he went further and further. By the middle of July he felt able to tackle the adventure, and they all agreed that he must put it off no longer. They had no idea how long it might take him to find his way into France, but he couldn't afford to be lost in the mountains when the cold weather started.

He could see that Marta was sad at the prospect of losing him. For nearly a year he had been part of her life, and she had lavished her skill, knowledge and tenderness upon him. He suspected that Gil too would be sorry to see him go. It was Gil's decision to bring him home in the first place that had saved his life, and he took some pride in the invalid's recovery. Angus, with his halting Catalan mixed with French had opened new doors for both his hosts. The exotic element that had come into their lives was about to disappear. Angus felt sure they would both miss him.

As for Quimeta, the best thing would be to say nothing about the impending departure of her idol. After the event they would tell her he had gone but would come back. They could only hope that the vagueness of her sense of time would keep her happy in the expectation of his return.

'I'll write as soon as I get to France,' Angus said.

Both husband and wife looked at him in some alarm.

'Oh, you can't do that,' exclaimed Gil. 'We never get letters here. Never. After all, we can't read or write. Poor country folk like us have hardly any schooling, and neither of us ever managed to make anything of this writing business. So we get no letters, and if a letter arrived for us at the village it would raise a great deal of suspicion. Especially a letter from abroad.'

Angus bowed to their decision. He had realized from the start that they were taking a great risk in sheltering him. Up till now their delicacy had prevented them from ever referring to this. Now they had been forced to do so by his alarming suggestion.

'So there's no way I can let you know that I've got through?'

Gil shook his head. 'It's just one of the things we have to put up with in our position. You people who live in a free country . . . '

Angus felt a great wave of sadness as he realized how final the parting was going to be. This meant that he would never be able to hear from them. He felt he could hardly bear it. These three people had been his whole world for nearly a year, and now he was going to lose them forever. But there seemed to be no alternative, apart from staying on here indefinitely, and he knew this was no solution, either for them or for him.

It was decided that Gil would set out with him early the following night and take him as far as a disused hut some ten miles along the track that headed north, where Angus would spend the rest of the night. After that he would be on his own.

The last day passed in a daze for the three adults. When Quimeta went off unsuspecting to bed, Angus found it hard to realize that he would probably never see her again. The still, beautiful face that he had gazed on with such pleasure would soon become a memory and nothing more. But he wasn't allowed to think about this for long. Soon Gil said it was time to go, and picked up the bag of provisions that Marta had prepared. Angus would have given anything to have some small object, anything, that he could hand over as a parting gift, but he had nothing. He was overwhelmed by a sense of his own poverty. These people had given him back his life, and he had nothing, nothing he could give them in exchange, not even the smallest token.

He turned to say goodbye to Marta. She was looking at him, solemn but serene. He wanted to thank her for all she had done for him, but no words came. In silence he held out his hand to her. Then, as mothers do with their children, she took his hand and guided it to make the sign of the cross. She stood at the door and watched till the men had disappeared in the darkness. Then she went into the kitchen and sat down in the chair that Angus had usually sat in. When her husband came back many hours later she was still sitting there. Gil could see that she had been crying, but she was now composed.

'All right?' she asked.

'All right.'

And they went to bed without exchanging another word.

Early in the morning they were awakened by a terrible shriek from Quimeta.

'He's gone,' she wailed, rushing into her parents' room. 'He's gone, he's gone, and I'll never see him again.'

They comforted her, assuring her that he would come back.

'When? Today?'

'No, Quimeta, not today.'

'Then tomorrow?'

'No, not tomorrow. But soon. He'll be back soon.'

After a few minutes Quimeta was reassured, and settled down with her doll.

Her parents looked at each other, and exchanged a sad smile.

5

After Gil left him in the hut Angus tried to sleep, but sleep refused to come. He was reliving the events of the past months too intensely to be able to relax. The thought that he would probably never see these people again filled him with sorrow and anger. It seemed monstrous that their lives should have been interwoven so closely only to be torn apart brutally and finally. His mind kept going over all sorts of ways of getting in touch; but, on examination, he found that they were not in reality feasible. As long as Franco was in power there was no hope that he would ever get back into the country – assuming he could get out of it in the first place. And he could foresee no possibility of a change of regime for many years to come. The country had been bled dry by the war. Where would anyone find the strength to oppose the victor now?

At last he fell asleep and woke up with a heavy heart hours later in the early-morning light. He was stiff from his long walk, but felt fit enough to continue his journey. As he walked he felt the weight of the recent past gradually lifting from him, and began to experience the excitement that starting a new phase in life usually brings.

And there was no denying that a slight sense of excitement

was fully justified in the circumstances. Perhaps even more than a slight one, he reflected ruefully. He had no idea what his chances of getting through to France might be, but he suspected they were rather slim. He was thankful for the experience of this type of terrain that he had gained during his first winter in Spain, while he and the little group of fellow volunteers had wandered through the mountains of Aragon. This time at least there was no snow. But there were other dangers. And this time he was on his own. He suddenly realized that never before had he been entirely dependent on his own resources for survival.

He walked on and on, guiding himself by the sun, and continually trying to work out the position of the different peaks in view, in case the sun should disappear. During the day the heat was pitiless, and he had to cover long stretches with no shelter of any kind. And, because of the altitude, the nights were unpleasantly cold. Only for an hour or two in the morning and in the evening was the temperature easy to bear.

To his surprise, he found that, in spite of the sorrow of parting from his friends, in spite of the hardships of the journey and the dangers and difficulties that lay ahead, he was enjoying himself. He had an active temperament, and the enforced idleness of the last months was something quite contrary to his nature. Looking back at that phase of his life, he felt surprised at the patience with which he had borne the inaction. Perhaps I'm learning, he thought. Or perhaps I'm just getting old. Not too old, he hoped, in view of the hazardous journey ahead of him. Then he thought of the models of patience and endurance with which he had spent all those months. Perhaps it wasn't so surprising after all that a little of those qualities should have rubbed off on to him.

He stuck to the high mountain tracks as long as he could.

But after a week he had exhausted his provisions, and hunger drove him down to the nearest valley. He had found out from Marta what the going rate was for simple things like a loaf of bread or a pound of tomatoes, and knew he had enough money to keep him going for some time. This was because his hosts had insisted on his taking the ambiguous two hundred pesetas. They had pointed out that this sum might mean the difference between life and death on such a journey, and he had yielded.

After a while his descent brought him to a road. It must surely take him to a town or village, he thought. There was little traffic about, and what there was passed him without stopping. The times were evidently too dangerous for people to be willing to stop for strangers.

At last he came in sight of a village. Quite a big one, it seemed, with a church perched on a little hillock in the middle, and the houses clustered round it. Must be big enough to have a shop or two, he thought, as he came to the first of the houses.

He passed in front of the church and stopped to have a look, in spite of his hunger. It was evidently very old – Romanesque, with a few later additions. After his sojourn in the tiny *masia* perched on the side of the mountain the church seemed wonderfully spacious, though it was only a modest *església de poble*.

He walked on till he found a baker's shop, then discovered to his consternation that it was closed. For a moment he wondered whether today was perhaps a holiday, then he remembered the disconcerting Spanish habit of closing all shops for a few hours during the heat of the afternoon. This was quite a blow. Not only did it mean he would have to go hungry for another hour or two, but it also meant hanging about the village, the very thing he was least anxious to do, as this would most certainly draw attention to himself. He could, on the other hand, just walk on in the hope of finding another village not too far along the road. But he was beginning to feel weak and faint with hunger, and he was afraid to set out in his present exhausted state on what might prove a walk of many miles.

He stood forlornly outside the baker's shop in this deserted-looking village, wondering what to do. Although there were no people in sight he suspected that eyes were staring at him from behind the net curtains of more than one window. He felt utterly alone and unprotected, and thought with longing of the safety of Gil's house. Once again he remembered the sadness of the parting from Marta, and seemed to see her farewell gesture as she guided his hand in the sign of the cross. And suddenly he knew what to do. The church, of course. He would take refuge in the church while he waited.

He knew that Spanish churches were always kept open, and walked confidently up the steps leading to the huge door with its iron studs. Inside, it was blessedly cool and almost dark. He could make out a few huddled figures kneeling before an image, and remembered to genuflect as he passed in front of the altar. Then he sat down on one of the wooden chairs near the back of the church.

As he sat in the cool half-light his thoughts went back to the significance of Marta's gesture. With the sign of the cross she had entrusted him to the care and protection of God – or, more probably, the Virgin. At the same time, by guiding his hand in the movement, she had underlined the mother-and-son aspect of their relationship. It had also been her way of showing him what seemed to her the true path.

Up till that time he had been touched by the gesture and impressed by its symbolism; but he had not been prepared to accept the idea that it might bear fruit in any way. He was not going to accept Roman Catholicism, not even for Marta's sake. Still less so now that the Church was so blatantly sharing in the triumph of Franco's victory. And yet the gesture *had* borne fruit, and in a surprisingly practical way. Its memory had given him the idea of seeking sanctuary in the church.

He had no means of telling the time. He would just have to hope that the shops would be open by the time he came out of the building. Meanwhile, he rested. When he did venture out he found that the shops were indeed open, and he bought some coarse dark bread, a pound of tomatoes, and some olives. He ate as he walked along. He could have bought white bread, but decided against it, as the other was cheaper, and looked more sustaining. He was in no position to allow himself to be swayed by gastronomical considerations.

Anyway, the bread tasted heavenly, in spite of its unprepossessing appearance. Suddenly there came back to him the old Scottish saying that he had heard in his childhood – hunger's good kitchen. Yes, he thought, that's perfectly right. It is the best sauce. Until this Spanish adventure he had never really been in a position to test the truth of the adage, never known what hunger, real hunger, was. And it struck him that much of our indifference to the suffering of others is based on sheer ignorance. Perhaps, he thought, if I'd known what it was like to have a craving for drink and be deprived of it, perhaps then I might have tackled the problems with Nancy in a different spirit.

The problems of the present situation soon drove everything else out of his head. He had decided that his best option was to follow the road right through the village and continue along it for some time, till he was well out of sight of the houses. He didn't want to be seen leaving the road in case this might suggest he was trying to hide. So he followed the road for another mile or two, then turned off on to a track that wound uphill towards the mountains. He would dearly have liked to ask someone how far the frontier was, but that was obviously out of the question. He would just have to struggle on in ignorance.

6

A few days later, with the bag Marta had given him for his food empty again, he stood looking down into a green valley with a large village or small town nestling in the hollow. He would have to risk going down. An hour or two later he was standing in a small grocer's shop, completing his purchases. With his replenished bag slung over his shoulder, and with the change in his hand, he turned round to leave the shop and found himself face to face with a couple of Civil Guards. One of them held out his hand.

'*A ver, la cédula*,' he said.

Reminded by the man's accent that most of the members of this force were southerners or Castilians, Angus didn't make the mistake of answering in Catalan. Besides, all officials insisted on Castilian as the language of the Patria.

'*No tengo*,' he said, determined not to show his passport unless absolutely necessary. He had heard too many tales about documents not being returned. Before setting out from Gil's farm he had decided on what story to tell in the event of being stopped by the authorities. Now he explained that he was a reporter working for an English paper. He had been sent over to cover the last stages of the Civil War, and had been injured in one of the final encounters.

Naturally they wanted to know where he had been ever since, and he told them that some monks from a nearby monastery had taken pity on him and looked after him till he was well enough to set out on the return journey. His money was running out, so he was having to walk back to France, where he had friends who would help him.

It was a feeble story, and he was not surprised when it was greeted with grave suspicion. After a few more awkward questions and unsatisfactory answers the guards marched him off to their headquarters and locked him up.

His cell was small, bare, and none too clean. It had one rickety chair in it, a heap of straw, and a small window with bars, so high that it showed nothing but a patch of blue sky. The same view as from his bed in the *masia*, he reminded himself. Only this time there was no Marta with her ministrations, and no Quimeta with her angelic smile. On the other hand, this time at least he wasn't injured.

So far.

He was anxious to know his fate, but nobody seemed to be the least bit interested. Eventually he managed to extract from his captors that it all depended on what the *sargento* decided should be done with him. And the *sargento*, it appeared, was away. And they didn't know when he would be back. When Angus insisted on trying to get more information from them about his probable fate, all they did was shrug their shoulders.

'Who knows?' they would say. 'Perhaps a few days, perhaps a few weeks.' Their philosophy seemed to be that there was plenty of time, and that their prisoner had nothing to complain of. Weren't they feeding him twice a day? Well then!

7

For several weeks Angus saw no-one but his two captors. He heard other voices, comings and goings in the Civil Guard headquarters, people walking along the street, snatches of conversation. Most of all he heard the two guards talking as they sat on duty in the hall outside his room. He soon learned to distinguish them by their voices, and determined to find out as much as possible about them simply from their conversation – partly as a form of amusement, partly because he felt that in his situation any information he could get hold of might eventually prove useful. The main difficulty, because of their strong Andalusian accent, consisted in actually making out what they were saying. Gradually he began to make progress, and soon had a rough idea of what they were talking about.

His guards were called Andresillo and Severo. He had no trouble establishing that much. But it took him some time to be sure that he'd got the allocation of their names right. In the end he had to accept that the portly middle-aged one was the possessor of the name in the diminutive form, while the slender young man with the melting brown eyes was Severo.

Andresillo always looked rather slipshod and was inclined to lounge about, mopping the sweat from his brow. Severo on the other hand was rather a dandy, and moved about with the studied grace of a *torero*. Angus had no doubt that he must be a huge success with the girls.

After the first few days both of them became quite friendly with their prisoner, and would sometimes open the door to let a little more air into his tiny cell, and would stand in the doorway chatting. Angus thought with wry amusement of the opportunity he was losing on these occasions. If I were a real he-man, he thought, I'd knock the two of them out and make a run for it. But his right arm was still very stiff and weak, and he knew he would get the worst of it in any scuffle that might ensue. And anyway, the men were armed. It would be madness even to think of it.

As time went on and their ability to talk together increased, he discovered he was beginning to like them, in a guilty sort of way. To feel nothing but scorn for a Civil Guard seemed to him the least that a decent man could do. And yet, he couldn't help feeling that these two specimens, though representing an evil and corrupt system, were rather likeable fellows in themselves. They told him stories about what was going on in the village, about how they had distinguished themselves during the Civil War, about their home towns in Andalusia. And, like most uneducated Spaniards, they systematically put the world to rights more or less every day. What the other countries needed – England, France, the lot – was a really strong dictator like Franco. That would soon settle things.

Or else they would expatiate on the beauty of the Spanish language, scenery, women, or anything else Spanish they happened to think of. At first Angus found all this distasteful and infuriating, and listened in pained silence. But it was all done in such simple good faith that he came to accept that there was no point in judging these people by the self-deprecatory standards in which he had been brought up. They might be insensitive, tactless, monumentally wrong, but at least it was all part of a yea-saying attitude to life. It occurred to him that they might have thought better of him if he had stood up for his own country, dwelling proudly on its virtues, instead of listening to their rodomontades in polite, palpably unconvinced silence.

It was a hot, still evening in August. The sun had set some time before, and darkness had fallen, but a heavy blanket of heat still hung over the little town in the hollow. The two guards were sitting just outside the open door of Angus's cell. The conversation turned on women. Andresillo was describing one of his amorous adventures.

'What a woman!' he said. 'What a woman! And she thought the world of me. Mind you,' and here he held up an admonitory hand, 'that was before I was married. Once you're married you have to settle down. That right, Severo?'

Severo, who had only been married a few months, seemed to think this was uproariously funny.

'Hair like jet, long enough to sit on,' went on Andresillo. 'And eyes, eyes like black fire! And her figure!' Here Andresillo held out both hands, cupped, well in front of his chest. Severo roared with laughter, and Angus permitted himself an appreciative grin.

'Look at him, just look at him!' bellowed Severo, pointing to Angus and digging his elbow into Andresillo's ribs. 'He knows what you mean, all right. He knows what we're talking about.'

Just then there was the sound of running feet in the street outside, followed by a series of shouts. The two guards rose as a man and rushed outside, leaving the cell door open. Cries of 'Stop thief!' could be heard, and more and more voices joined in the uproar.

Later on, Angus looked back with astonishment at the coolness with which he had seized his opportunity.

As soon as his captors had rushed out he picked up his one possession, the bag Marta had given him, and he walked out into the hall. The front door was open, and through it he could see a lot of people rushing past. At the other end of the hall he saw an open window and opted for this, in the hope that it would lead to a quiet back street. He had just jumped out of the window when he heard the guards coming back. Looking round he saw that he wasn't in a back street at all, but in an enclosed garden with a ten foot wall round it. Crouching behind a bush he listened to the conversation of the guards as they discovered his absence, blamed each other, and decided to set off in his pursuit.

'*Por aquí, por aquí*,' exclaimed Severo, and rushed towards the window.

'*No, hombre, no!*' Andresillo insisted that Angus must have escaped into the street and joined the crowd. 'Come on,' he said, 'we've got to follow him. There's no time to lose.'

Severo was still in favour of trying the garden first. Peering through the bush, Angus caught a glimpse of Andresillo grabbing Severo by the arm and dragging him out of the front door.

He gave them a few seconds, then climbed back into the building and followed them out into the street. The crowd had stopped a little further down, and the two guards were pushing their way through. Angus set off in the opposite direction and turned into the first side-street. Near the end of the town he came across a small shop that was still open. He knew he couldn't afford to waste any time, but he also knew there was no point in heading for the mountains with absolutely no provisions. He bought as much as he could carry, blessing the inefficiency of the guards that had allowed him to keep his money and his bag.

The following day was almost like a holiday. It was wonderful to be out in the fresh air again, to see the mountains, to be able to move. But his spell of captivity had reduced his stamina, and he found he had to take it easy, for he tired readily. So he had plenty of time to think over the events of the past weeks.

The more he thought about it, the more he felt inclined to believe that the guards had connived at his escape. Whether they had acted in collusion, whether each had decided separately to give him a sporting chance, or whether it was Andresillo alone who had engineered things so that the prisoner could get away, he was unable to decide. He even wondered whether the whole business, from start to finish, had been a put-up job. Had someone been induced to raise the alarm by crying 'Stop thief!' simply to create a distraction and give the guards the opportunity to rush off leaving his cell door open?

That too was a possibility, though less likely. He had been in Spain long enough to know that the average Spaniard is perfectly willing to ignore the law if it runs counter to his own ideas; and he felt reasonably certain that his captors had come to harbour feelings of friendship for him. It was clear that their post was not run on particularly strict lines – after all, the *sargento* had not yet put in an appearance. It was possible that the two men had decided they could get away with a little leniency, provided it was disguised as an accident. Surely even officialdom must look on inefficiency as an eminently human quality, and therefore forgivable.

Whatever the truth of the matter, he hoped that the two men wouldn't be too severely reprimanded for letting him get away. But that was yet another thing he would never be able to find out. Marta and Gil, whom he would never be able to see or hear from again, and now these two men who had arrested him and then shown him kindness. And in this case he would never even be able to determine the extent of their kindness.

8

One thing Angus had managed to find out from the guards
was that the village was only some twenty miles from the
frontier. Perhaps in another two or three days, if all went
well . . .

It would have taken him only one day if he had dared to
follow the road. But going by road was much too dangerous,
and would inevitably have led him to a frontier post, with
Spanish *carabineros* demanding to see his documents. No,
the only thing for it was to head for the mountains again and
try to get across at some wild and uninhabited pass.

By the third night he felt he must be getting quite close,
and a great wave of excitement ran through him as he thought
that by the following evening he might be a free man. When
he woke up in the morning his excitement was considerably
dampened by the presence of a thick mist. He could see no
more than a few yards ahead of him in any direction. And the
most disturbing thing was that he wasn't at all sure of which
way to head in the first place. He had made his bed among
some bushes in a little gully, after making a mental note of
the lie of the land so that he would have a clear idea of which
direction to set off in.

Now his landmarks were all gone. Once again he had to

decide between two dangers. If he set off he might find he was going the wrong way. And if he waited for the mist to clear, well, that might take days, and he would have no food left by then. In the end he decided that he'd had a lot of waiting to do during the past year, and that action, even if perhaps not the right action, was more in keeping with his character. He then reflected rather ruefully that action, especially if it turned out to be the wrong action, was the characteristic thing for him to do.

At first things went well — assuming he was going in the right direction, and that remained to be seen. He noticed that the track he was following was getting steeper and steeper. Perhaps this was a good sign. Perhaps it meant he was on the central ridge of the mountains. He wished he had spent more time studying the map of the Pyrenees. But the last time he had had access to a map had been in Paris, when he had no reason to imagine it would ever be of such vital importance to him. And during his stay in the *masia*, when he knew how useful it would have been, there was no map available.

After a while he noticed that the track seemed to have disappeared. This had happened quite often before, and he had always been able to find another sooner or later, so he wasn't too perturbed about it. But this time the mist kept him from getting an overall view of his surroundings, and he was unable to decide which were the likeliest places to make for.

He wandered on in increasing despondency, aware that the landscape seemed to be getting sterner and more forbidding. He could only make out the contours of the rocks and slopes nearest him, but what he saw was not reassuring, and the terrain was getting rockier and more difficult all the time. He stopped to take counsel with himself and came to the conclusion that he'd better turn back. He felt certain that he must have climbed too high and missed the pass. He certainly didn't want to enter France by climbing over the top of one of the peaks.

As he turned, his foot slipped on the scree and he lost his balance and fell. The slope was so steep that he began rolling down, unable to stop. Bruised and battered, he came to a halt on a rocky ledge about six feet wide. Above him was the steep slope he had just rolled down. Below him was a thick mass of mist. He had no means of assessing how deep the chasm below him might be, but he was sure it was a long, long way to the bottom.

For the first time he considered the possibility of giving up. Perhaps the best thing would be just to lie on this ledge till he died of starvation or exposure. Or perhaps he would be found by some friendly shepherd who would rescue him. During the whole of his journey he had kept a look out for any lonely figure to be seen on the mountains, and avoided the few he had come across. There certainly hadn't been many of them, and it struck him now that this very place was the least likely to produce a fellow human in any form. He had obviously wandered far from any sort of a track, and no-one was going to find him here on his rocky ledge.

So, for all practical purposes, he could dismiss the idea of rescue. That being so, he had two alternatives – either lie here, giving up completely, or pull himself together and find a way back to more manageable terrain. And then he thought of a third possibility. The quickest and simplest thing of all, the one involving least effort, was simply to roll over once more in the same direction, and that would put an end to all his problems.

He considered all three possibilities in a surprisingly detached manner. There was a lot to be said for the last option. It avoided the need for any further effort, and at that moment he felt intensely weary. Just one final decision, he told himself, and that's the end of the struggle for ever more. And he wondered whether that was what Nancy had felt when she jumped from that fifth-floor balcony. It would be funny if he chose the same form of death as she had.

And why, after all, shouldn't he? What was there in his life to make it worth the effort of struggling on any longer? He decided he was going to examine the situation as dispassionately as possible, as if he had been consulted by someone else who was faced with these doubts and difficulties. The practical man in him still kept his options open, reflecting that there still were many hours of daylight ahead of him. He could afford to lie there for an hour or two getting his priorities right and still have time to find his way back to safer ground if he decided against the tempting chasm below.

Let's go back to the beginning, he thought. And the beginning was one of his earliest memories: the Shetland pony.

When the pony arrived they were told it was for him and his brother Gavin to share. At first they were given rides turn about, held on by one of their parents. It was wonderful. Soon they were both anxious to ride without help. No, they weren't big enough yet. Then one day Gavin was allowed to ride on his own. But when Angus claimed his solo ride he was told he would have to wait.

'But Gavin's riding alone. Why can't I?'

'You're too young. Gavin's a year older.'

And that, thought Angus, was that. There was no arguing against it. He recalled the bitterness and the sense of injustice that this had awakened in him. And then he remembered Bob's suggestion that all the bitterness he still felt was really directed against Gavin. He still found this hard to accept, but decided to look at the rest of his life with this possibility in mind.

Throughout his childhood this sense of being discriminated against for no fault of his own had been with him. As they grew older, and he realized that Gavin's position as heir marked him out for privileges that could never fall to the younger son, his sense of injustice increased. Thinking it over now, he realized it was a wonder that he and Gavin had got on as well as they did. They had been together till the war separated them. After that their paths diverged completely.

Angus had always assumed that he had decided to stay on in France simply because he liked the people, the language and the way of life. But was it perhaps, as Bob had suggested, because this was a way of avoiding Gavin's ever-present superiority as far as their position in the family and in society in general went?

Suddenly his mind flew forward a few years to the brief but devastating episode in which he and Meg had nearly become lovers. He had never been able to explain this incident satisfactorily to himself. His pity for Meg in her childlessness was perhaps not the only reason. Now he began to wonder whether his secret motivation had been an unconscious desire to get his own back on Gavin.

He left that thought in brackets, as it were, and went back to the time he had spent in Paris after the war. A good time, full of artistic and intellectual discoveries.

There was an openness about Paris in the twenties, with its endless possibilities, that seemed magical after the enclosed atmosphere of Kintalloch. These were exciting years, and he had felt that for the first time in his life he was enjoying real freedom. At home, at school, in the Army, he had always had to fit in with the desires and demands of others, always in a subordinate position. In Paris he was his own master, working as a freelance.

And this was when women began to play an important role in his life. He had often wondered why he always seemed to get involved with the helpless, pathetic sort of woman. Up till this moment he had found no reason for this tendency. He now saw that this fitted in very well with the new view of himself that he was exploring. Being the saviour and protector of some helpless woman was the very thing to compensate for his years of dependence and subordination. So all these women, including Nancy, had appealed to him precisely because of their distress! He had seen himself, as they had seen him, in the glorious colours of the hero whose strong right arm was there to protect them. The situation, he realized now, had a destructive mechanism built into it. For, once the maiden had been rescued and the dragon destroyed, the whole situation was altered. The hero's help was no longer required, and he stopped being a hero in the woman's eyes. In short, his heroic quality was only circumstantial, not intrinsic. The fact that the affair with Nancy had lasted so much longer than the others, even before their marriage, was probably because her weakness for drink had kept them together, simply because it was a weakness, and so left her vulnerable.

The thought of Nancy always brought with it feelings of sorrow and guilt. But this time, lying precariously on his mountain ledge, he felt he was beginning to understand things rather better. Understanding, he told himself, always seems to come too late. Even if he were to survive the present danger, he was too late to do anything for Nancy.

But for Louis?

Was it too late to do anything about the animosity that divided him from his son? Suddenly his mood changed as he relived that last, painful scene. Once again he saw Louis's white, angry face, as he asked his father why he kept coming back to Kintalloch. Angus had replied that it was because he loved and missed his son, to which Louis had retorted that he neither loved nor missed his father. And then he had added:

'And what's more, you're not my father. Uncle Gavin's my father. I know that sounds silly, but you know what I mean.'

And Angus had known perfectly well what he meant.

He had then asked the boy whether he would rather he stopped coming, and Louis had preserved a sullen silence. Again, Angus had known what he meant. He had sworn that he would never go back. The memory of this bitter little exchange was enough to drive away all the vision and self-knowledge that had come to him in his meditation.

His intention had been to continue his inner exploration right through the recent past and then try to assess what his prospects for the future might be in the event of his getting out of this place alive. Now, with the memory of Louis's rejection fresh in his mind, it seemed to him that there was no point in the exercise. There was really nothing in his life worth living for.

He opened his eyes and saw that the mist had cleared. Instead of being able to take any comfort from this, he discovered that his situation was even worse than he had thought. He was now able to see clearly just how terrifying his surroundings really were.

Looking down into the chasm below he realized that it was much deeper than he had thought, a narrow cleft between huge black rocks, with a dark stream studded with white waterfalls below. Behind him was the steep slope he had rolled down, crowned by an enormous mass of almost black rocks towering up to the sky. In front of him, on the other side of the ravine, was an equally high and even more threatening cliff face. The gorge was so narrow that the cliff on the other side, which looked almost concave, seemed to be leaning out over him, as if trying to meet its partner on the opposite side. Angus felt utterly engulfed between the two huge dark masses.

For the first time in his life he experienced a sensation of cosmic evil. Ill-will seemed to emanate from the towering rocks above and the dark chasm below. It was as if he were about to be swallowed up and utterly destroyed by this mountain which had split open to suck him in.

He felt so totally annihilated by the violence of his surroundings that he lay back again and closed his eyes, convinced that he would never move again. Well, he thought, that's it. All that effort for nothing. This is the answer. I can forget all about the past and the future, and what I should have done and what I might yet do. All I can do now is lie here and let the evil take over.

With this surrender came a great feeling of detachment and peace. It seemed as if time had stopped. He remembered feeling like this while watching the falling snow in the Aragonese mountains, and felt as if he could almost hear Bob's voice again as he spoke of those moments that seem to go on for ever. And Bob had said that they could come even in the midst of the horror and tragedy of the Civil War. Now, surrounded by this sense of an evil that seemed to emanate from the tormented landscape round about him, he felt the same timeless peace and detachment flowing into him. He had no idea where this peace came from. It just seemed to be the natural outcome of his surrender and acceptance of things as they were. The peace and the evil flowed together, and he neither sought the one nor rejected the other, but accepted both.

He never knew whether he had actually fallen asleep. But he became aware of a feeling of warmth permeating him. He opened his eyes and saw that the clouds had gone. The strip of sky between the two huge rock masses was blue, and the sun was shining down on him. He felt refreshed and ready to take another look at how he might escape from this Dantesque landscape. He stood up and looked about him, determined to examine all the possible routes. There was no point in looking downwards. Nothing but a sheer drop to the bottom of the chasm. If he took that direction it certainly wouldn't be from choice. All his defeatist feelings had left him. No question of suicide as the easy way out, he decided.

Looking along the ledge on which he stood he saw that it narrowed gradually in the direction from which he had come, eventually disappearing entirely. So, if he were to turn back, as had been his intention when he had fallen, he would have to scramble up to where he had been then. That would certainly be dangerous, and not very profitable even if he managed it. He would be unlikely to retrace his steps without another fall – and there was no guarantee that the ledge would stop him this time. The only possibility seemed to be to follow the shelf in the opposite direction, in the hope that it would lead him out of the chasm.

As he continued along the shelf he began to realize that there seemed to be a recess in the rock-face to which the ledge clung. When he got to that point he discovered that it was more than a recess. The rock-face was, in fact, cut off at right angles, revealing a gentler slope on the side now exposed to him. The going would be difficult, even dangerous, but at least a fall would not plunge him down to the bottom of the ravine he had been perched above for so long. And he would no longer have the sensation of being devoured by the two towering rock masses. As he left the gorge behind him he noticed with relief that he now had an open outlook, and a distant view down to a flatter, greener landscape.

Advancing slowly and carefully, he made his way down the steep slope. There was still a lot of scree about, and on several occasions he was only saved from a fall by finding a solid piece of rock to cling to. He persevered, taking his time, inching his way down to the green valley below.

He was still far from this promised land when he stopped suddenly, listening. From somewhere below, a thin, clear, melancholy sound rose up to him. Looking carefully, he managed to distinguish a figure down below, outlined against the green of the valley. In the clear mountain air the sound of the shepherd's pipe was carried up to him across the distance.

9

The man stood still as he played, with his sheep grazing on the slopes about him, and Angus stood still too, listening and watching. He felt as if he had just wakened from a terrifying nightmare and found himself in the middle of Arcadia. After the harshness of the rocks that had surrounded him the green of these lower slopes looked incredibly soft and tender, the motionless figure seemed poised with an infinite grace, and the sheep appeared as gentle, rounded forms, artlessly scattered about in a delicate and shifting pattern. Most enchanting of all was the thin, clear stream of sound that rose from the shepherd's pipe.

Angus listened in a still ecstasy.

It seemed to him that all his sufferings were amply repaid by the beauty of the moment.

The music stopped, and the figure began to move away.

Angus was jolted out of his blissful dream. He started hurrying down in pursuit, but soon realized that he could never hope to catch up. There was at least a quarter of a mile between him and the shepherd, and most of it was still the steep, rough shingle of the upper slopes, which made it impossible for him to hurry. He had no idea whether his voice would carry that distance, but he knew he must try. He stood still, took a deep breath, and shouted as loud as he could.

The man stopped immediately and turned round, then began to advance towards him. Angus hurried on to meet him, till he found his strength suddenly giving way, and he sat down and waited. The shepherd continued to advance, unhurried, and at last Angus was able to make out the features of an elderly man with a weatherbeaten skin furrowed in a pattern of fine, deep wrinkles. He was small and wiry, and moved effortlessly up the steep slope till he came to a halt a few feet from Angus. The two men gazed at each other in silence for a few moments. Angus was so relieved at having escaped from the menacing jaws of the gorge that he had completely forgotten about the other dangers that possibly still threatened him. He had no idea whether this man would look upon him as a friend or as a foe. It all depended on what country they were in.

The man spoke first, and he spoke in French. It took Angus a little while to realize the significance of this.

'How did you get here?' was the man's first question.

Angus turned and pointed to the entrance to the ravine from which he had just come.

'Through the Devil's Gorge?' The man looked at him incredulously.

'Is that what they call it? I'm not surprised. Yes, that's the way I came.' Angus had slipped into French without even noticing. Suddenly he realized what language they were speaking.

'So we're in France?' he asked.

'Yes, my son, we're in France.' The man nodded and smiled, then said, 'We've been getting more than one coming over from Spain in the last few months. But no-one has come through the Devil's Gorge. I didn't think it could be done. Why on earth did you take that route?'

Angus explained about the mist. 'I'd have turned back right away if I'd seen where I was. By the time the mist cleared it seemed easier to go forward than back. But for a long time I thought I was never going to get out.'

'You wouldn't have been the first man to die in that place. And I'm sure you're the only one that's ever got right through. The Holy Virgin has been watching over you.'

The words brought back a vision of Marta teaching him how to make the sign of the cross, and he felt a lump rising in his throat. And the thought of Marta brought the more mundane memory of the bag she had given him. To his surprise he found it was still slung over his shoulder. He realized now that he had had nothing to eat since first thing in the morning. This had, no doubt, contributed to the weakness that had overcome him and forced him to sit down.

'I've got some food,' he said, opening the bag and taking out a very stale piece of bread and a few olives. He offered some to the shepherd, who shook his head:

'No, I've had mine. When you've eaten, we'll go down to my hut – if you can get that far. It's about two miles from here. All downhill, and no gorges,' he added with a smile.

On their way down the man explained that he spent all summer on these higher slopes with his flock, living in a hut on the side of the hill. Then, when autumn came, he went back down to join his family on a little farm near one of the mountain villages. Angus had learned about transhumance many years before from a Spanish friend who had taught him one of the folk songs of these wandering shepherds. He asked his companion whether he knew it.

'No. Let me hear it.'

Softly, slightly hesitantly, Angus sang the first verse:

Ya se van los pastores
A la Extremadura.
Ya se queda la sierra
Triste y oscura.

'A fine tune,' pronounced the man. He then took his pipe out of his pocket and began to play the melody he had just heard. Angus was filled with admiration.

'You're very gifted,' he said.

'It's my one talent. And I'm very grateful for it. There are times when it can be lonely out on the mountains. And then I take my pipe out and, *voilà*, there are two of us.'

Angus spent several days living in the shepherd's hut. He was so tired that he slept all night and much of the day. It was an ideal place to recover from the strain and exhaustion of the long march. In the late afternoon he would set out to meet the shepherd as he came down with his flock, and the two men would walk back together as they had on that first day. Angus's face and hands had been badly cut and bruised as he rolled down the steep slope to his lifesaving ledge, and his host insisted that he stay till he looked and felt a little more normal. It was a welcome respite, before tackling the problem of finding his way to Toulouse, where he hoped to get in touch with his friend Tim Baker.

One evening, as they sat at the door of the hut watching the lengthening shadows, Angus asked, 'Why do they call it the Devil's Gorge? Just because it's so dangerous?'

'No, not just that. There are plenty of other dangerous places in these mountains, places that would kill a man. And they have killed many, many. But the Devil's Gorge is worse than dangerous.' He paused, then went on, almost apologetically. 'We have stories about these places, our people here. Stories that would seem mere foolishness to an educated man like you. But they mean a lot to us. They help us to understand, you see? And so we have a story about the Devil's Gorge. But it would seem mere foolishness to you.'

'Tell me, please.'

'Well, it all goes back to the origin of the Devil. You know that Satan rebelled against God, and was condemned to live in Hell for all eternity. And that was perfectly right and just. God is always just. But he is also merciful. And so he took pity on Satan, and agreed to let him have one way, one way only, to come up to earth every so often, when the longing for our green fields and blue skies became more than he could bear.

'And God chose this place, this mountain, for him because it was so far away from everything else, with nothing but other wild mountains anywhere near. God thought the Devil would be able to get up to less mischief here than anywhere else. So he commanded the lightning to strike and split the mountain in two, to let the Devil come up for a breather, you might say. Well, the Devil was very glad, *ça va sans dire*. But, being the Devil, it didn't occur to him to be grateful. It simply didn't strike him that he was morally bound not to take advantage of this privilege. After all, you can't really expect much moral sense from the Devil. And the Good Lord, who is, *bien entendu*, perfect, but who does have his little moments of distraction, simply forgot that the Devil could hardly be expected to play the game.

'And so the Devil was coming up every day, if you please, and going further afield than he should, and getting up to all sorts of mischief. So much so that all the priests in the country got together – and it takes a lot to get them to do that, I can tell you – and sent a delegation of angels to the

Almighty, asking him to do something about it. What they wanted was for the whole gorge to be sealed up, so that the Devil would never be able to come up here again. But God said that he couldn't possibly do that. He had given his word to the Devil, and he couldn't go back on it, even if the Devil was taking unfair advantage. He had promised to let the Devil come up for air, and he refused to take the privilege from him. After all, as he pointed out, where would we be if the Devil could accuse God of perfidy? We might as well give up the whole idea of right and wrong, of good and evil, of justice and mercy. The priests simply wouldn't know what to preach, and all the angels would be out of a job.

'So God had a good long think about it, and in the end he came up with His solution. The gorge was to remain, so that Satan could come up when he really needed to have a look at the blue sky. He could go to either end of the gorge and have a good look at the green fields of the valleys below. But an angel with a flaming sword was to stand at either end of the gorge and refuse to let the Devil past him, whatever he might say. And that's the way it's been ever since.'

Angus smiled. 'I saw no angel,' he remarked.

'But you felt the evil?'

'Yes, I felt the evil. And, who knows, perhaps it was one of the angels who helped me to get out.'

'There you are, you see? God knew what he was about, after all.'

'But what about all the other people who have died there? Did the angels not notice them?'

The shepherd appeared to consider the matter, then answered with a twinkle in his eye:

'The angels too have their moments of distraction.' Then, in a more serious tone of voice, he added:

'I think you must be a good man. That is why God has

protected you. That is why the Holy Virgin has watched over you.'

It was quite dark by now. Angus sat at the door, looking out into the blackness, thinking of all the dangers he had been through and wishing he could believe the shepherd's solution to the riddle of his survival. What was it that had protected him? For the shepherd it was God and the Virgin. And Marta would surely have given the same answer. As an educated twentieth-century agnostic the only answer Angus could come up with was Blind Chance. He reflected that it wasn't much of an answer. Simply another way of saying, We don't know.

He said goodbye to his new friend with almost as much regret as he had felt in parting from Gil and his family.

Only here there was nothing so crushingly final about the parting. There was no reason why he should not come back again some day. He could even keep in touch with the shepherd by letter, though Alphonse confessed that his writing was a bit *comme ci, comme ça*.

They parted one morning at the door of the hut. After shaking hands formally the shepherd turned to go. Then he thought better of it, came back and embraced Angus. '*Allez, allez,*' he said, then set off towards the higher slopes, leading his flock.

Angus looked with affection at the hut that had been his home for a while, then, with a last look at the slight figure trudging up the hill, he set off.

His idea was to go and see his friend Tim Baker in Toulouse, borrow enough money to get him to Paris, and then work at any translating or teaching he could find at short notice till he had saved enough money to take him to England. He was anxious to go and see Dick's parents, in the almost forlorn hope that they might have some news of their son. Then he must somehow find Bob's parents. It was not an interview he was looking forward to, but it had to be done. He had promised.

Beyond that he could form no plan. Probably he would settle down in Paris, as before. Every time he thought of Kintalloch and his desire to go back and take his share in its daily life, the thought of his son's stern face as he repudiated his father came between him and any softer images. Whatever happened, he felt he simply couldn't go back there. By now they must all have given him up for dead. Let them go on thinking it. For Louis, at any rate, he was convinced that this would be the best solution.

10

Tim Baker was crossing the hall of his house when he heard the phone ring. He picked up the receiver and said:

'*Allô!*'

'Hello, Tim. This is Angus speaking. Angus Lindsay.'

'Good God, Angus! Where are you?'

'I'm at the station here in Toulouse. Can I come and see you?'

'Yes, of course. Come right along.'

'Fine. By the way, you may get a bit of a shock when you see me. I've been in the wars.'

'That's all right, old chap. Not the first time, is it?'

Tim and Angus had fought together in the trenches during the Great War, and had kept up the friendship for some years. Tim had married a French girl and settled in Toulouse, where his father-in-law found a place for him in his export business. Then, when Angus married Nancy, they had stopped seeing each other. Claudine had made it clear that she was not prepared to have any dealings with a demimondaine like Nancy, even if the couple were, at long last, respectably married. Over the next few years the men had continued to exchange letters, but with decreasing frequency. And when he joined the International Brigade, Angus hadn't got round to writing to Tim with the news. But he was sure his old friend would be willing to help him out, especially now that there was no fear that Claudine might have to be brought into contact with the discreditable wife.

When Angus rang the bell Tim himself opened the door. He was obviously very much taken aback by his friend's appearance.

'I say, you *have* been in the wars, haven't you?'

'Yes, quite literally. I've just come from Spain.'

Claudine had appeared at the other end of the hall. She failed to recognize Angus at first. Then she gave a gasp and advanced, holding out an uncertain hand. For the first time Angus realized just how battered and tramp-like he must look. In the big, expensively furnished hall of the luxurious villa he felt distinctly out of place. He had forgotten how well off these people were.

It soon became clear that the most urgent thing was to get him upstairs and made presentable before any of the servants saw him. Before he had been able to tell them any more than that he had just walked across the Pyrenees, he was soaking in a hot bath and Tim was laying out a complete outfit for him from his own wardrobe.

Less than an hour later he joined them for drinks out on the terrace, feeling strange and inhibited in his borrowed plumes and new surroundings. The house seemed far too big and ridiculously sumptuous.

His friends listened with some concern and some disapproval as he told his tale. After all, joining the International Brigade was surely a bit off. Going off to fight for the Reds in Spain! Angus tried to explain that he hadn't really seen it that way. He had gone because he felt useless and unwanted at home. It had been, he was now willing to concede, more a gesture of protest than an expression of his deepest convictions.

'Rather like joining the Foreign Legion, you mean?' suggested Tim.

'Yes, something like that, I suppose.'

He hurried through the tale of his adventures as quickly as he could. It was obvious that his hosts weren't really terribly interested, that their minds were on other things.

As soon as he could decently change the subject, Tim broke in with:

'There's going to be a war here, you know. I don't suppose you've heard much of what's been going on, but the situation is really serious.'

'Any day, but any day, we may be at war,' broke in Claudine. 'It is terrible, really terrible.'

Angus agreed. Yes, war was a terrible thing. All that loss of life . . .

'Ah, but you've no idea how it's going to affect us. It will spell the death of the export business.' Claudine was evidently very worried.

Angus felt a slight sense of shock on realizing where their priorities lay. Then he reminded himself that they were talking about the family business, with which Claudine's whole life was bound up.

'It's going to cost us thousands upon thousands,' added Tim.

Angus tried to show rather more concern than he actually felt.

Early in the evening he pleaded his exhaustion as an excuse and retired to bed, sick at heart. He was shocked by the contrast between the abundance with which his friends here lived and the poverty from which he had just come. And he was even more dismayed by the narrow, self-centred outlook that had been revealed to him. Here we are, he thought, on the brink of a major war, and all these people can think of is their reduced profits. Perhaps we deserve a war.

He had known almost nothing of the international situation during the past year, though from what little he had been able to gather from Gil's reports he could see that things were not going well. But all the same it was a shock to realize just how bad they were.

As the couple sat having their final drink before going to bed, Claudine said:

'It's a pity about Angus, isn't it?'

'Yes, he seems to have had quite a rough time of it, poor chap.'

'That wasn't what I meant. I'm thinking of the future, not the past.'

'Can't say I know what you mean, my dear.'

'Well, look at him now. Here he is, forty years old, with nothing, but nothing, to his credit. He's going back to Paris to live in some miserable little flat, earning a pittance as some sort of a language teacher. He's not made very much of his life, has he?'

Tim felt a bit stung on his friend's behalf, and rose to his defence. 'Well, he's lived, hasn't he? Perhaps a bit more than most of us.'

Claudine shrugged her shoulders. 'He's got nothing to show for it.'

Tim spent a restless night. On the one hand, there were all the fears about the war and how it would affect their business. Even though these fears had been pushed into the background by his friend's return, they were still there, weighing heavily upon him. And on the other hand he felt diminished in comparison with Angus. He would certainly not have had the courage willingly to choose the freedom and poverty and adventure that had fallen to Angus's lot; and yet he felt intensely aware that there was a dimension missing from his own way of life.

The following morning he drove Angus to the station to get a train for Paris. 'We must keep in touch, now that you're back,' he said.

'Yes, we must,' Angus replied with little conviction. He knew it would be churlish to show his disappointment in the man. After all, he had helped him out, insisted on his keeping all the clothes he had provided from his wardrobe, lent him more money than he needed to get him settled in Paris. But he couldn't help feeling that the warmth had gone out of their friendship. They no longer shared the same outlook on life that had drawn them together in the trenches. He knew they had both moved on from there, but in different directions.

'You know, Angus, I was thinking, after you'd gone to bed last night, you've had quite a rum life, haven't you?'

Angus smiled. 'I suppose you could say I have,' he conceded.

'And it just made me think . . . Well, my life's been rather settled, you know. I mean, I got married nearly twenty years ago, moved into the outfit, and it's all gone quite smoothly since then.'

Angus caught a slightly plaintive note in his friend's voice. 'You're not complaining, are you?'

'N-n-no, not complaining. But somehow . . . Well, what I mean is, you only live once, don't you? And sometimes I wonder if I've ever really lived at all. Since we got out of those trenches, that is. See what I mean?'

'Yes, I see what you mean. Your life's been eminently successful – wife, children, lots of dough . . . But perhaps a bit dull?'

'Perhaps just a little. But that's not the point I was trying to make.'

'Well, what was it, then?'

Tim scratched his head. 'It's hard to say. I'm not really very clear about it myself. But your visit has left me with the suspicion that I'm missing out on something. And I don't quite know what it is.'

Angus thought for a moment. 'That shepherd I was telling you about last night,' he said.

'The one you stayed with in the mountains, you mean? What about him?'

'He had nothing. Or practically nothing.'

'Are you preaching communism to me?'

'No, I'm certainly not preaching communism. It's just that he was the happiest-looking man I've ever seen.'

'Well then, you're preaching holy poverty, like St Francis.'

Angus shook his head. 'I'm not preaching anything. I'm just trying to find out what the missing element is in your life. And in mine.'

Queer chap, thought Tim after he had seen Angus off. I wonder whether his experiences have unhinged him a bit. And yet . . . He sighed, shrugged, and then stopped to buy a paper. The news was worse than ever.

11

Angus had been looking forward to seeing Paris again, and decided to walk from the station to his friend's flat. He had nothing to carry, it was a pleasant evening, and he had plenty of time. But he didn't enjoy the walk as he had expected. The place seemed far too big, and hideously overpopulated. I'll have to get used to city life again, he thought. I've been in the wilderness too long.

And then it struck him that, even if he wanted to live in the country, he had no way of earning a living except in a city. He thought of all the tiny villages and solitary farmhouses he had seen on both sides of the Pyrenees, and had to admit with regret that he couldn't possibly earn his living by teaching languages in such surroundings. No, there was no place for him in the country. Except at Kintalloch, of course. That was the one rural place where he could earn his living, helping with the estate.

But Kintalloch was out of the question.

Well, if it had to be a city, there were worse places than Paris, he thought, as he wandered along the banks of the Seine. He had lived there for so long that he knew the city well, and yet it was so big that there were always new places with little surprises to be found.

He was in no hurry to get to his friend's flat, for he remembered that Pierre, also a teacher, often taught till well into the evening. But about nine o'clock he turned away from the river and made his way to the Rue des Francs-Bourgeois. Pierre's flat was in one of the oldest buildings in the street. As he climbed up to the top storey he noticed with satisfaction that nothing seemed to have changed. The lighting was as poor as ever, the paintwork as chipped and shabby as before. Probably not a desirable quality for the inhabitants, but reassuring for him in his unsettled state.

He reached the top landing and rang the bell. The door was opened almost at once by a tall, slim girl with dark hair and eyes. Angus was taken aback, then decided that this must be the latest girlfriend. Not bad, he thought appreciatively. Pierre always did have an eye for a pretty girl, and this one was a stunner.

'Is Pierre at home?'

'No. They don't live here now.'

'They?'

'Pierre and his wife, my sister Annette.'

'Oh, I didn't know he was married.'

'Yes, last year. Are you a friend of his?'

'I'm Angus Lindsay. We used to teach together.'

The girl's face lit up on hearing the name. 'But come in! Why didn't you say so right away?'

She stepped back to let Angus into the tiny hall. He remembered the flat well – a small sitting room, one small bedroom, a smaller dining room with a little slice of kitchen attached, and a minute bathroom. And a view over the rooftops of Paris.

'So you live here now?' he asked, once they were seated.

'Yes. Pierre and Annette moved to Toulouse, and I took over the flat here.'

'That's ironical,' he said with a laugh.

'Is it?' She sounded surprised.

'About Toulouse, I mean. I've just come from there.'

'Oh! You look as if Toulouse hasn't treated you very well.' She was looking at the scars and bruises from his fall in the Devil's Gorge.

'I don't think we can blame Toulouse for that. I've had other adventures.'

'Tell me.' The girl sat back ready to listen to a long tale, then suddenly jumped up. 'But you must be hungry, if you've come all that way. I'll get you some food and you can tell me all about it while I'm preparing the meal.'

She took him through to the dining room, pulled out a chair from the table and turned it to face the kitchen door. 'Now you can talk while I'm busy in the kitchen. *Allez, racontez.*'

Even though the girl was busy with her preparations, Angus could see that she was paying far more attention to his tale than it had received in Toulouse. And he was left with the impression that the mention of the International Brigade elicited nothing but approval on this occasion. So much so, in fact, that he began to feel he was gaining her admiration under false pretences. I'll have to tell her, he thought. I'll have to explain that I went there for personal reasons rather than out of political conviction.

The explanation, and the meal, and the coffee in the sitting room afterwards, and the full account of his adventures since leaving Paris, took up a long time. Suddenly Angus realized it was after midnight.

'It's getting late. I must go.'

Marie stood up too. 'Where are you going? Do you have somewhere to sleep?'

Angus hesitated.

'You have nowhere to sleep,' the girl stated. 'You thought Pierre would put you up, *n'est-ce pas?*'

'I gave up my flat when I went to Spain,' he said.

'Then you must stay here,' she said firmly. 'So there's no hurry. Sit down again and tell me more.'

Angus sat down again, but insisted that it was now time for her to tell him more about herself. 'All I know is that you're called Marie, that Pierre has married your sister, and that you now live here. That's not nearly enough.'

She explained that her family lived in Rouen, where she had been brought up, that she worked as a secretary in a government office, and had moved into this flat when Pierre left because her own flat in the Quartier Latin was even smaller and really rather horrid.

'So this is luxury to me,' she said. 'For Paris, that is. At home in Rouen we have a nice big house with a garden. But in Paris, you know, we are all like this—' and she held out her hand with the fingers all squeezed together. 'And that's all there is to tell,' she concluded. 'I have had no adventures. Well, not the sort you have had. My adventures have been – emotional, shall we say?'

Angus hoped she was prepared to embark on another emotional adventure. He knew how straight-laced the provincial French could be; but this girl seemed rather more *parisienne* than *rouennaise*.

'I was in love with your friend for a while. That's how he met my sister. And after that he decided he prefered her.'

'Were you very upset?'

'Of course. One imagines that the end of the world has come. But, *tout passe!*' After a pause she said, 'And you? There have been many women in your life?'

Angus nodded. There had indeed been many women in his life. After Nancy's death he had sworn he would keep away from the species. But eventually he started having the odd affair, always with women he didn't really care about. He was determined not to get involved again.

'Yes, there have been many women in my life. Too many.'

'Is that a warning?'

'It was meant as a warning – to myself.'

'And are you going to heed the warning?'

He shook his head. 'Not unless you want me to.'

In answer she took his face in her hands and began kissing the scars and bruises. 'Your poor face,' she said. Then she kissed him on the mouth. 'And the warning?'

'Let's forget about the warning. Besides, it's different this time.'

'It's always different,' she said.

'Well then, *vive la différence!*'

Later that night, lying in bed beside the sleeping Marie, he came to the conclusion that it really *was* different this time. For once he was not playing the saviour. Rather, their roles had been reversed. In this relationship it was evidently Marie who would take the lead. And this time perhaps it would work out all right, because she was a natural leader. Before, he had always appeared to be the stronger character. But he was not really meant for the part, and sooner or later the whole thing had broken down. In Marie he sensed a much stronger character than his own. It would be a relief to let her take the lead.

They spent the following day in the flat, mostly in bed. On the Monday morning Marie went down to the shops for provisions before going out to work. She came back looking pale and shaken.

'It's war,' she said.

'When was it declared?'

'Yesterday. And we spent the day in bed.'

'We didn't know.'

'We should have known. We knew how grave the situation was — or I did, anyway. We could at least have listened to the radio.' Suddenly she turned round with a look of alarm on her face. 'Will they call you up? Will you have to go?'

'I shouldn't think so. I'm forty years old, and disabled. My right arm and shoulder are pretty useless. You saw the scar. I don't think anyone would want me.'

'I want you.'

'I hardly think that will influence the authorities, one way or another. But they might find my languages useful.'

'Of course! Why didn't I think of that? One of the government offices, perhaps even mine. They're sure to be looking for translators and interpreters. I'll make inquiries this very morning. And now I'd better go, or I'll be late.'

Angus never found out whether the office she worked in was really looking for new translating staff, or whether she had used her powers of persuasion on her chief, but the following day he was called for interview, and by the end of the week they were both working in the same building.

Angus felt he could really have done without this war. After all, it was his third, and he had become increasingly convinced that war solved no problems. All it did was create new ones. However, this was a matter he hesitated to take up with Marie, who had wholeheartedly embraced the cause of her country.

Marie normally lived with great intensity. Since the arrival of Angus and the declaration of war she had been living at fever pitch. She felt that her life had suddenly been raised to the level at which all life should be lived. Here was a man who was truly worth loving, a man who had lived his life fully, who had travelled, who had fought for his principles — for she refused to believe that Angus had only joined the International Brigade out of pique. That was obviously nothing more than the typical English understatement, of which one heard so much. This was a man who could change the direction of his life at a moment's notice.

How dull and unadventurous and conformist all the men she knew seemed in comparison, even those she had loved. Take Pierre, for instance. Married to her sister and settled in a good teaching post in Toulouse, from which nothing but this newly declared war could ever hope to save him. Doomed to a comfortable *vie de province* for the rest of his days. And if she had married him, that would have been her fate too. No, she felt sure that such a marriage couldn't possibly have lasted. But it might be all right for Annette, who demanded less drama and less heroism in her life. Annette's standards, Marie felt regretfully, had always been rather low.

The first months of the war, the phony war, exasperated her intensely. She longed to be at Hitler's throat. What were her countrymen thinking of, sitting back doing nothing? Life in Paris went on much as it had before the declaration of war, and Marie was in a fever of impatience. Her only consolation lay in the happiness of having Angus to love. She suspected that her lover was perhaps a little more content with the slow pace of the war, but decided not to make an issue of it. She was sure that, once things started happening, he would share her enthusiasm.

But the winter dragged on, and spring arrived, and still nothing seemed to be happening. One day, when Marie expressed her impatience to Angus, he pointed out that as long as things remained as they were, they could stay together. 'Once the war really gets started there's no knowing what may happen. Meanwhile, we've got each other. And I know I've never had so much in all my life.'

She looked at him with glowing eyes. 'Yes, it's wonderful, being with you. I've never known anyone like you.' Suddenly she laughed. 'You seem so quiet, so *posé*, and yet you've been through so many adventures. Don't you miss your adventurous life, living here so quietly with me?'

'Living with you is the biggest adventure I've ever had. And the nicest. On the whole adventures are not particularly pleasant.'

She looked at him seriously. 'You think I'm a bit childish, don't you, with my longing for action?'

'No, not childish. But young. I think it's just that I'm getting old. I would give anything in the world to know that we could go on like this, sharing this happiness. And I can't think of any kind of adventure that wouldn't put that in peril. I want this to go on for ever and ever.'

She put her arms round him and sighed. 'Ah, if only there were just the two of us! But there are so many other things that we can't help belonging to. There's France, and England . . . '

'And Scotland,' he put in.

'I'm sorry, I forget. Your country and mine, your people and mine. And if we don't do something, Hitler is going to swallow us up.'

'When the time comes, we'll act. Your country and mine, you and me. I promise you. Only, I'm not looking forward to it. I know what it's like. You're too young to remember the last war. I've been in two so far, and I've really had enough.'

'But when the time comes, you'll take action?'

'I've promised. I'll do whatever is required.'

They didn't have much longer to wait. When the Germans

attacked the Low Countries in May, Marie was ecstatic. Soon her people would be mobilized. Soon the Germans would be fleeing. But as the enemy swept forward and took Sedan, Marie was filled with dismay and incredulity. The French defences at the Meuse had crumbled. The day Pétain took over, Marie and Angus held a personal council of war. They knew that the new leader favoured an armistice with the Germans and that it would only be a matter of time till this was concluded.

'We're not going to sit here doing nothing, are we?' she asked.

'No. I, for one, probably won't get the chance. After all, I'll be considered an enemy alien.'

'You'll have to go into hiding?'

'Or face internment. For those who want to resist, going into hiding is the only way.'

'Then we'll go together.' Marie's eyes were sparkling with excitement.

Angus felt he was being dragged out of the apathetic mood that had possessed him since coming to Paris. Up till now his happiness with Marie had been so great that he had found it impossible to think of anything else. Now, his habitual buoyancy returned to him, and the prospect of a total change of scene became immensely attractive. If Marie was with him, it would be all right.

12

That evening Marie's parents sat in their pleasant sitting room in Rouen and hoped their daughter wasn't too upset at the news. They themselves weren't feeling any too happy about it. But they were older, and had learned to take things less to heart than their daughter.

M. Mercier had retired from his position as bank manager the previous year, and had been feeling a little aimless ever since. The long wait of the phony war had done nothing to raise his spirits.

'Well, my dear,' he said to his wife, 'the news is bad, very bad. I'm afraid things are going to get worse, much worse. But we got through the last war, and no doubt we'll get through this one.'

'Not everyone gets through.'

'That's true. But as long as the young people survive — our young people. I suppose that's as much as one can ask.'

'I wouldn't actually mind very much if we survived it too, if you don't mind,' put in Mme Mercier with mock acerbity.

They heard the front door being opened and looked at each other, smiling.

'It must be Marie. No-one else comes in without knocking.'

'Good. We've not seen her for a long time.'

At this point the sitting room door opened and Marie came in. Instead of going over to kiss her parents she stopped at the door and said:

'I've got someone with me. Can I bring him in?'

'*Mais, naturellement!* What a question!' Marie's parents were used to the succession of admirers that she was in the habit of bringing home.

Marie pulled Angus into the room and introduced him.

'He's English – I mean, Scottish.'

'British, then?' suggested her father.

'Yes. That's why I've brought him.'

Her parents didn't appear to see the connexion, but greeted Angus politely while waiting for an explanation.

Marie looked at them with a mixture of tolerance and impatience. 'You don't see why, do you?'

Both parents shook their heads.

'Well, you know what's happened, don't you? Pétain's taken over. That means an armistice with the Germans. We'll be on their side, can you believe it? And *they* won't,' and she pointed at Angus, who felt he was being called upon to represent his whole nation.

'Quite so,' said M. Mercier. 'That puts monsieur in a difficult position,' he conceded.

'It puts him in an impossible position,' declared Marie. 'That's why I've brought him here.'

'Quite so, my dear. I see the problem is that monsieur will be considered an enemy alien. But as much so in Rouen as in Paris, don't you think?'

'Quite so,' mimicked Marie. 'But the problem is that I can't hide him in Paris.'

There was a pause during which the parents exchanged startled glances. Then they both shrugged their shoulders at the same time. Angus didn't know how to interpret this shrug, but Marie evidently did, for she rushed forward and kissed both her parents.

It was Mme Mercier who spoke, turning to Angus. 'Our house is at your disposal, monsieur. We know that our daughter would not bring anyone here who was unworthy.'

Angus had felt acutely embarrassed during this exchange. It was now a relief to be acknowledged as a participant in the conversation. He had tried to get Marie to see her parents first and explain, but she had refused, on the grounds that the safest thing was to smuggle him in as quickly as possible. Later he was to come across other examples of this *fait accompli* technique of Marie's. He accepted it as a proof that hers was the dominant character.

He now thanked his hosts, who responded by assuring him that his French was wonderfully good.

'It's his job,' Marie explained.

'To speak good French?'

'Yes. I teach French to the English and English to the French.'

Marie cut short any further polite exchanges by offering to show Angus 'his' flat. 'I've told him about the flat upstairs,' she said to her parents. The flat consisted of a large room that had been the schoolroom of the two daughters, and a small bedroom, kitchen and bathroom for the governess. After the girls grew up it was never used except for the occasional party.

Marie was in her element. 'You realize this is going to be dangerous, harbouring the enemy? It means that Angus mustn't move out of the flat, not even to come downstairs, except at night, with the door locked and the shutters closed. It doesn't matter if they see me. I've a right to be here.'

'But you're going back to Paris, surely?' suggested her

mother tentatively. Neither parent was ever anxious to cross their daughter.

'No. I'm staying here with Angus. Upstairs,' she declared belligerently.

Reluctant as he was to consider the possibility of a parting, Angus had begun to realize that it would be unwise for Marie to disappear from the Paris scene just as he was about to do so, and had suggested as much to her in the train. Marie was adamant. Nothing was going to be allowed to separate them.

But her father put his foot down. If Marie left the job without warning there would be inquiries which would almost certainly lead to her home in Rouen. Altogether it was much too dangerous. She must continue working in Paris for some time at least. She could then hand in her resignation, pretexting family commitments. But unless she promised to go back to Paris the following morning by the very first train, her parents would feel obliged to refuse to conceal her friend.

Marie put up a good fight, but in the end had to yield to her father's unexpectedly firm resolve. It was not often that Marie's wishes were ignored in that family. She only yielded on condition that she should come home every weekend.

'Yes, dear, certainly,' said her mother, 'it will make such a pleasant change.'

Marie had the grace to look slightly guilty. 'I know. You can blame him. I couldn't leave him, could I?'

'No. But you could have brought him here before now. Then we could all have had the pleasure of each other's company.'

After Marie left in the morning, Angus spent a long time meditating upon the fact that he was once again a prisoner. First in Gil's house, then in the headquarters of the Guardia

Civil, and now as the concealed guest of a virtually unknown couple. This time, at least, he hoped to lead a less idle life than on the previous occasions. The Mercier parents had agreed to do whatever was necessary to establish contact with any anti-German activities in which Angus could join during his incarceration. They had no doubt that some form of clandestine press would soon be set up, and felt sure that Angus could play an important part in this.

So life settled down into a quiet routine for Angus. M. Mercier lost no time in establishing contact with early pockets of the Resistance movement, and it wasn't long before Angus was handling much of the copy intended for the clandestine press. As the humiliation of the German occupation made itself felt with increasing rigour he began to wish he could play a more visibly active part. But at least he felt he was doing all he could in the circumstances, and Marie was satisfied. This was as important to him as the desire to help his country and its allies.

During the early months, while Marie continued to work in the government department, she felt extremely frustrated.

'Mind you,' she said to Angus and her parents one day, 'don't forget I'm doing my little bit. You've no idea how many things go wrong in the office now. I lose files, my typewriter breaks down, I forget about important appointments . . . In short, I'm not half such an efficient secretary as I used to be.'

'With a bit of luck they'll sack you,' Angus teased.

'How I wish they would! Then I could come here and do something more than the little bit of stealthy sabotage I'm indulging in now. You don't know how lucky you are, you three. You're all doing something really worthwhile.'

'It's your father who is doing all the business of establishing the contacts, and Angus who is doing all the writing and editing. I'm doing nothing,' said Mme Mercier. And there was a note of real regret in her voice.

Marie got up and went over to her mother. She put her arms round her and kissed her. 'You're the one who is making it all possible. How do you think these two helpless males would get on without you? You're utterly indispensable.'

'After all,' said Angus, 'if my presence here is discovered, or if they get any idea of what we're up to . . . '

' . . . they're not going to believe that you of all people, knew nothing about it, are they?' M. Mercier then turned to Angus. 'You have no doubt found out already that not a fly dare move in this house without permission from my wife.'

Some weeks later Marie told Angus that she could no longer stand the strain of separation from him. 'It would be bad enough if things were safe and peaceful,' she said.

'If things were safe and peaceful we'd be together all the time. No need for separation then.'

'Well, they're not, and I can't stand it any more. Every time I go back to Paris and leave you behind I think – this may be the last time I see him. Anything could happen, to you or to me. And I can't bear the thought of not being with you if anything goes wrong. So I've decided I'm coming home for good, very soon.'

'Marie, darling, is that safe?'

'Is anything safe? Look, Angus, they've forgotten all about you now, after all these months. If I go away, it won't look suspicious any longer. And you needn't argue with me, for I've already handed in my resignation. Oh, I've done it all very skilfully, don't worry. All the inefficiency I was telling you about, it served two purposes. In the first place it gummed up the works a little, and in the second it got me into trouble with the boss. So I explained that I was worried about my mother's health, and that I'd been coming home to Rouen every weekend because of that, and that I wanted to hand in my resignation to be able to go home and look after her. And he accepted it. So I'll soon be home for good. Beside you.'

Angus was moved and alarmed at the same time. He suspected that, freed from the long hours of work in the office, Marie would take a far more active part in the Resistance movement, and he feared for her safety.

'My darling Marie,' was all that he could say. There was no point in arguing. The decision had been made, without consultation. Once again he was overcome by the conviction that Marie's was by far the stronger character. He simply had to accept her as she was, loving her and fearing for her.

'Have you told your parents?'

'No, not yet. I thought perhaps you might tell them after I've gone to Paris.'

Angus laughed. 'So there is someone you're afraid of? You little coward. So I'm to break the news, am I? I'm to bear the brunt of their wrath.'

'But darling, they can't possibly blame you for what I've done.'

'They might think I'd put you up to it.'

This time it was Marie who laughed. 'They know me too well. And by the way, will you remember to tell *Maman* she's suffering from a dangerous heart condition? Just in case they make any inquiries.'

The following day Angus felt some trepidation as he prepared to tell his hosts of their daughter's decision. He started off with a tactful reference to the way he thought Marie was suffering from the separation from her family under the German occupation.

Mme Mercier looked at him in some amusement. 'From her family? Oh yes, that's why she comes here so often, isn't it, Edmond?' She turned to her husband for confirmation.

'Yes, indeed,' he agreed. 'We've noticed how devoted to her family she's become since this gentleman came to live here. A mere coincidence, *bien entendu*, but most gratifying.'

Taking advantage of the indulgent and playful mood in which his hosts appeared to be, Angus went ahead and delivered his news. The reaction was not as dramatic as he had feared.

Mme Mercier limited herself to saying, 'Well, I hope it's not premature.'

Her husband shrugged his shoulders philosophically and murmured, 'She has always been *très volontaire*. Pig-faced, you say in English, no?'

'Pig-headed, actually.'

'Ah, yes Pig-headed. Face, head . . . quite a difference, *n'est-ce pas?* A little more than a nuance, yes.'

Angus then told Mme Mercier that officially she was suffering from a serious heart condition.

'*Tiens!*' remarked that lady. 'And I never felt a thing. I suppose I'd better remember to get a bit breathless when I'm out shopping. Will that do, do you think?'

Her husband was shaking his head. 'No, I think we'd better do the thing properly. A visit to our good friend Dr Leroy might not come amiss. I really think your medical practitioner should be informed, just in case they decide to do a bit of checking up.'

Mme Mercier smiled indulgently. 'Thorough, isn't he?' she said turning to Angus with a nod towards her husband. 'Next thing, he'll be asking me to do breathlessness practice, just to make sure I do it convincingly.'

'I'm glad you don't suffer from *suggestibilité*, my dear. You might end up quite neurotic.'

Angus was profoundly thankful for the high spirits and good humour that his hosts so often displayed. After all, his life was extremely limited, and he saw no one but the family, a very few trustworthy friends, and the fellow conspirators with whom he worked. The latter were a mixed bag, united only by their desire to thwart the Germans and a consciousness of the dangers they were running. Conversation with them was therefore never relaxed nor wide-ranging. But the Mercier couple had a sense of fun that even their difficult circumstances seemed incapable of extinguishing, and an ironic turn of phrase that delighted Angus.

Before Marie's arrival the following weekend they told Angus that they meant to play a little trick on their daughter.

'So don't be alarmed. Marie knows what we're like, and she'll soon get the point.'

As soon as Marie appeared, looking as if she rather doubted her reception, Mme Mercier put her hands to her breast, leaned against her husband, and began to pant violently. For a second or two Marie stared at her mother in alarm; then she burst out laughing, rushed forward and flung her arms round both her parents. All three collapsed on to the sofa, laughing helplessly. And that was how they settled the matter of this particular *fait accompli*.

Marie was overjoyed at having given up her work in Paris. 'It's wonderful to feel I'm not working for them any more,' she kept on saying. 'Not that I worked all that well, to tell the truth. And I'm sure they'll have no trouble in finding someone else equally inefficient.'

'Intentionally, do you mean?' asked Angus.

'Well, perhaps. Or perhaps simply with a natural aptitude for inefficiency. I suppose either will do equally well for our purpose.'

Angus was delighted to see her looking so happy. But in spite of the joy of seeing her every day and sleeping with her every night, he couldn't quite repress certain misgivings, and tried to get her to promise not to get too involved in the more dangerous aspects of the Resistance. She usually put him off with an 'I'll be careful', or something of the sort.

But one day, when her eyes were brighter than ever with repressed excitement, he decided to pursue the matter further.

'Look, Marie,' he said, 'I can see perfectly well that you're more involved in this than you're prepared to admit. Don't you see that you're taking advantage of the fact that I have no means of finding out exactly what's going on?'

Marie looked rather taken aback:

'You think I'm being unfair to you?'

'Well, what do you think? Are you sure you're concealing nothing from me?'

Marie suddenly burst into tears. 'Oh, why does it have to be like this? I belong to you completely, body and soul, you know I do. But if I'm going to do anything for my country, you know how it has to be. Absolute secrecy, or else we throw away lives needlessly. You know that nothing else would persuade me to keep anything from you.'

'I know, I know. And I'm not asking you to give away secrets. All I'm trying to get from you is a promise that you won't get involved in anything too dangerous.'

'But, my darling, it's *all* dangerous. What you're doing, what my parents are doing, what I'm doing. Would you like me to try and stop you, persuade you to hide here safely till it's all over, without taking your share of the work? You know that's not the kind of man I could ever love. So why ask me to be that kind of woman? Would you love her as you love me?'

Angus felt defeated. Marie's sense of the heroic was such that he was sure she would despise him if he told her he would love her just as much without her fierce patriotism. All his background and upbringing told him that women should be protected, that they should take no active part in the horrors of war. He tried to explain this to her.

'You mean the only part we should play is that of victim? Because we all have to play that part, like it or not. The bombs land on us just as much as on the men.'

'You know I don't mean that. There's a lot women can do without getting involved in the fighting.'

'Yes, stay at home and bear children for the next war, like the German women. That's what Hitler expects his women to do. Is that to be my role?'

For the first time Angus felt his anger flaring up against Marie. He moved towards her furiously, his fists clenched.

'Of course it isn't, and you know that can't possibly be what I mean. You're twisting my words, just to get away with your point of view. Sometimes I think it's all a game to you. You're like a gambler who can't keep away from the gaming table. I can see how it goes to your head. The more danger you get, the more you want. That's not patriotism, it's self-indulgence. You're like a child that won't give up its toy. And perhaps this toy's a bit more dangerous than you think.'

Marie's eyes flashed angrily. 'You mean that I wouldn't do all this if I realized just how dangerous it is? Is that what you mean?'

'Of course not.'

'Well, that's what you implied. And if you don't mean that, what exactly do you mean, may I ask?'

Suddenly Angus felt all his anger draining out of him, leaving nothing but a blind misery and apprehension. He sat down and took hold of her hand.

'Marie, I simply can't bear the thought of losing you. I mean I can't bear the thought of your being in danger when I'm not there to protect you. Can't you see? The whole world would come to an end for me if anything happened to you.'

'But the world has come to an end, Angus. The decent, normal, predictable world. You don't know what it's like out there, with *them* about. They are evil, evil to the core, and if we don't stamp them out we don't deserve to live.'

Angus looked at her glowing eyes and her flushed cheeks and realized there was no point in further argument. As well try to argue with a volcano, he thought.

Later that day, when they had got back on an even keel, Marie suddenly burst out laughing. 'It was wonderful to see you angry, Angus. Even though it was me you were angry with, it was wonderful all the same.'

Angus smiled and shook his head. 'You're incorrigible. I've never known anyone with such a thirst for violent emotion.'

'I have a thirst for life, that's all. And anger is a part of life, so I need my share of that too.'

'I'll remember. If ever I find you looking bored I'll know what to do.'

'But I'm never bored when I'm with you, my darling. So you can keep your anger for other people. I'll enjoy watching it.'

In spite of his worry over Marie's safety, Angus was happy during this stage of his life. It's funny, he thought. If anyone asks me when I'm an old man what were the happiest years of my life, I'd have to say they were the years shut up in a flat in Rouen, hiding from the Germans.

He had found that the only way to cope with the knowledge that Marie was in constant danger was by taking each day as it came, and giving thanks every time he saw her return safe and well. Once he spoke to Mme Mercier about this. He was impressed by the calm with which she took the situation.

'You have to remember this is not my first war,' she said. 'Marie's father was in the trenches right through the First World War. He was in the battle of the Somme — one of the few survivors.'

'I remember that. I was still at school, dying to be old enough to be sent out to fight. I felt that missing the Battle of the Somme was a personal disgrace.'

Mme Mercier smiled. 'Then you know how Marie feels. She has a high sense of honour.'

'Too high, I think at times. Don't you?'

'Perhaps too high for her safety. But not too high for her integrity.'

'And that's what really counts, isn't it?'

'It's the essence of Marie,' said the woman. 'We cannot ask her to be other than she is. One has to accept.' After a pause, she said:

'I sometimes think Marie is like a candle, a tall, straight candle that burns very bright. My other daughter, Annette, sheds a sweet and gentle light. Her flame does not burn so bright, but it will last longer. And they are like that, as the Good God made them. We cannot choose what our children will be like. We have to accept them as they are.'

Angus thought of his son, and wondered whether he had ever really tried to accept him as he was. Then his thoughts flew back to Marie.

13

Antoine was already waiting in the little wood when young Gilbert arrived. It was obvious from the start that there was something wrong with the boy.

'What is it, Gilbert? You look ill.'

'I am ill. That's what I've come to tell you. I can't go.'

'But if you're well enough to come and tell, me you might as well go. The whole thing will only take half an hour.'

'I can't go, I tell you.' Gilbert's voice sounded almost hysterical.

'What's the matter? Nerves? We all get them at times. You'll be all right once we get started. It's a bit like sitting an exam – butterflies in the stomach till you start writing, then it's all right.'

Gilbert shook his head. 'I can't go,' he repeated.

They stood in silence till they heard the car drive up. It stopped beside the two men and Marie got out.

'All right?' she asked. 'The material's in the car, ready for you to drive off.' The plan was for Marie to come in the car, into which the explosive had already been loaded, and leave it for the two men. She was then to walk back to Rouen. After the bridge had been blown up, the men were to abandon the car in some convenient spot not too far from the city. It was a familiar routine, and had proved very successful so far.

'Well, Gilbert?' said Antoine. 'All set?'

The boy shook his head. 'I can't go.' The others could see that he was shuddering.

'What's the matter?' asked Marie.

'Nerves. He'll be all right once we get started.'

'Nerves?' Marie sounded both incredulous and disapproving. 'There's no place for nerves in this job.'

Antoine looked at the boy with pity. 'It happens to us all at some time or other,' he said apologetically.

'Does it?' Marie looked at him defiantly.

Antoine scowled at her and put his hand on the boy's shoulder. 'Come on, lad, we'd better be off.'

Gilbert looked up imploringly at the two of them. Then he gave a loud, choking sob, and ran off into the thickest part of the wood. Marie and Antoine looked at each other in consternation.

'What do we do?' asked Marie. 'You can't go alone, can you? It would take too long. That would make it too risky. The guards would see you before you'd finished the job.'

'And there's no point in going if we don't finish the job. You either blow up a bridge or you don't. Half measures are no good in this sort of business.'

'I'll come with you.'

'No, that won't do. We'll just have to put it off.'

'But you know we can't. The others are counting on us. I'm coming with you, that's all there is to it.'

Antoine knew Marie well enough to realize that that was indeed all there was to it. Silently he got into the car and opened the passenger door for Marie.

'You'll have to tell me what to do,' was all she said.

They sat up all night waiting for her. It was foolish, they knew. What difference could it make? And yet they sat up, telling each other that there must have been some delay. They didn't know where she had gone, or what she was planning to do. There was nothing they could do except wait.

In the early hours of the morning they heard the familiar scratching sound on the back door, and rushed to open it. Antoine stood on the threshold. There was blood on his coat.

They dragged him in and shut the door.

'And Marie?'

Antoine shook his head. Then he pointed to the blood on his coat. Slowly, as if in a daze, he explained what had happened.

'The youngster,' he said. 'He just couldn't come. His nerve failed him. So Marie said she would come with me. I tried to stop her, but . . . Marie . . . you know! Well, we got it all done and she was great, as if she'd been at it all her life. And then, just as we were driving off, a guard appeared. I knew the bridge was going to blow up at any minute. Our only chance was to drive like hell. A few shots were fired, and I drove on till we were out of range. Then I stopped. Marie was breathing in an odd way, sort of gasping. And she said something. "Like Maman," she said. I don't know what she meant. And then we heard the bridge blow up, and she gave me the most wonderful, radiant smile.'

'And then?'

'And then she died. And I left her in the car and walked back. What else could I do? If I'd brought her back here in the car it would have incriminated everyone.'

A few days later Angus walked into the sitting room where Marie's parents were sitting in grief-stricken silence.

'I've come to say goodbye.'

'But you can't leave here. It's dangerous.'

'Dangerous? Do you think that means anything to me, now that Marie is dead?'

'It would mean a lot to her. She valued your life more than her own,' pointed out her father.

'I think she would approve of what I'm going to do. I'm going to join the *maquisards*. There's a lot going on down in the south.'

'I know. But you may never get that far.'

'That won't matter. I've nothing to lose.'

As he set off he remembered his words to Bob. Looking for a bullet, he thought. I really believed I was unhappy then. It seemed to him that never before had he had the slightest inkling of what loss or unhappiness could be.

What added to his grief was the feeling of intense resentment he felt against Marie for throwing her life away so light-heartedly. She had even died with a joke on her lips. Like Maman, she had said, thinking of her mother's mock breathlessness when she had pretended to be suffering from the heart condition Marie had invented for her. She had no right, he thought, she had no right to throw her life away. She knew how precious it was to me. His pride was deeply hurt. She had made it finally and irrevocably clear that she valued her country more than his happiness.

At other times his grief was unmixed with resentment, and his mind would dwell on images of Marie in all her more enchanting aspects – Marie laughing and joking with her parents, Marie sliding down the banisters like a schoolgirl, Marie teaching him the old French folk songs she had sung since her childhood; Marie under the shower, dragging him in beside her even though he was fully dressed.

And always her vitality, her zest, her intense determination to live life to the full. He remembered her mother's prophetic words about the candle, the tall straight candle that burns very bright. Well, the candle had burnt itself out, and left nothing but darkness.

It was months before his grief over Marie's death allowed him to feel the joy of being out in the open again after his years of captivity. And even then, the joy was tinged with the sadness of not having her there to share this freedom with him.

He spent the rest of the war fighting with the *maquis* in the South of France, in a sort of mechanical daze. He felt he was putting just about as much enthusiasm into it as Marie had put into her job with the Vichy government.

All the time he had the pervasive sensation of being a spectator, watching his own life in a detached, slightly bored manner. He was fighting not out of any strong conviction of his own, not even in the hope of killing Germans. He was fighting because he could think of nothing else to do with his life. And also, perhaps, because this was what Marie would have approved of. But he wasn't at all sure that he approved of it himself. Deprived of Marie's impetuous enthusiasm, he began to feel once again that war was a stupid business, and that it solved no problems. But he felt too uncommitted to anything, even to his own opinions, to do anything about it.

His recklessness in the face of danger won him the admiration of his comrades, who failed to see that it simply formed part of an all-embracing indifference. When he tried to identify the state of mind he was in, all he could think of was the word 'numbness'.

14

Claudine Baker sat in the bow window of her dining room, looking out on to the wilderness that had been her well kept garden, and thought about the changes of the last few years. The one thing that had sustained her through the disasters that the war had brought had been her conviction that things would get better once it was all over. The war had lasted a long, long time, and it had been even worse than they had feared at the beginning. But it was over now – well, the war was over, at any rate. There were other things that could never be put right.

But the one thing that could certainly be improved now was their financial situation, provided the right measures were taken without delay. And yet that was the very thing that Tim was refusing to do. Well, perhaps not actually refusing, as he kept insisting. He was just doing nothing about it. Which came to the same thing.

Looking at the abandoned, devastated garden, it seemed to her that it was an apt symbol for her whole life. And the house was no better. Everything in it seemed old and shabby. The gold paint was flaking off everything – the picture frames, the furniture, the elaborate ceilings. The marble floors were scratched and chipped. Nothing had been polished for years, and there was dust everywhere.

The situation of the family was even worse. The eldest son, Gaston, had been killed during the German advance at the beginning of their offensive in 1940. Their daughter, Monique, had run off with the penniless son of a refugee family from Spain – a family of no position even before the Civil War. Claudine had no reason to assume that his situation had improved in any way, but she knew nothing. After a disgrace like that the only thing one can do is sever all connexion with the offending party.

That left only the youngest son, Marcel. And last year, at the age of eighteen, he had started to cough up blood. They had sent him to a village in the foothills of the Alps; but so far he was showing no signs of improvement. Claudine kept on reminding herself that TB is a very slow business. In time he would improve; he must improve. Surely God didn't mean to take all three children from her?

As if all that weren't bad enough, there was the disastrous financial situation. The war had made things in the export business just as difficult as they had feared. And then, precisely when the situation was about to get back to normal with the forthcoming end of the war, her father had taken a stroke and died within a few hours. That left Tim in sole charge of the business. It was a golden opportunity for him.

But somehow he didn't seem to be keen on taking it. Now, with the war behind them at last, she had already had to point out to him several times that this was the moment to renew his contacts, to write to all his previous customers throughout Europe. If he didn't, others would. She knew what the business world was like. And Tim should know it too, after all those years working with her father.

But Tim seemed absent and apathetic.

I must speak to him again, she thought. I really must get

him to understand. You'd think the sight of this place in its present state would spur him on to action. But he walks about as if he didn't see a thing. I don't know what's happened to him. Right up to the moment he died, my father was more wide awake than Tim is now. And yet he was nearly eighty years old.

Claudine had grieved decorously over the death of the father she had lived with all her life. But the grief she had felt over the death of the senior partner in the firm had been of a different and more violent kind, a sort of desolation, alarm and foreboding all rolled into one. Of the four men in her life, the only one effectively left to her was her husband, and he seemed a broken reed.

She stretched out her hand as she sat at the window and touched the thick brocade of the curtains. Ten years ago these curtains had been her pride and joy. She had chosen the material herself in one of the best shops in Paris, and had had them made specially wide, so that the deep rich folds of the material hung down the walls at all the windows, giving a sumptuous appearance to the room. Now they looked faded and lifeless, all their dressing gone from them. The edges, scorched by the sun, had become so fragile that they had shredded into ribbons. The pelmets hung squint, and here and there the hem had come undone, leaving the curtain to trail on the ground. These curtains had been the focal point of this splendid room, whose walls had been covered with paper carefully chosen to set them off. Now they were the personification of faded splendour, the embodiment of decay.

Claudine sighed.

She stood up and walked over to look in the huge mirror that hung on the wall. It told her much the same story. Her beauty was fading too. The years had been as unkind to her as to the house. And for much the same reason, she thought – too many hardships, not enough care, too little money to cushion the passage of time.

She heard the front door being closed.

'Tim!' she called. 'Is that you?'

For answer Tim came and stood in the doorway of the dining room.

'Have you written those letters yet?' she asked, trying to sound as unconcerned as possible.

'What letters, my dear?' Tim too was trying to sound unconcerned.

Claudine's attempt at sounding detached collapsed. 'You know perfectly well what letters I mean,' she snapped.

'Oh, those!' Tim was still trying to sound casual.

'You mean you haven't.'

'I didn't say I hadn't.'

'Well, have you?'

'No, not exactly.'

'Am I to take it you've written them inexactly?' his wife asked scornfully.

'Now, now, my dear, there's no need to be flippant about it, you know.'

'Flippant! Me! You're the one who fails to see what a desperately serious matter it is. It's you who is throwing away our whole future with your indifference and procrastination.'

'Now, now, my dear,' Tim repeated. 'There's no need to take things *au tragique* like that. I haven't forgotten. I'm giving the matter some thought.'

'Thought! There's no need for thought. What we need is action. And quickly, or it will be too late. What could be simpler than to write to these people and tell them we're in business again, and hope to receive orders from them? What's so difficult about that? Why all this prayer and meditation?'

'Actually, I said nothing about praying. Might not be a bad idea, all the same,' he added, half jocularly.

Tim was in a quandary. His delaying tactics were not due entirely to apathy. He had several reasons for hesitating before embarking once again on large-scale business undertakings. For one thing, there was the sheer effort involved. It had been bad enough when things were going well, before the war, with Claudine's father at the helm. And Tim had always acknowledged that it was the old man who did the largest share of the work. But it wasn't only the volume of work that intimidated him. There was also the remorseless social round that success in business seemed to drag inevitably with it. It had all seemed to make a certain amount of sense then, before the war had brought other preoccupations. For one thing, there were the boys. In time they would take their place in the family business. It was worth making an effort to preserve it for them. He liked the idea of continuity, of preserving this business that had been in the family for over a hundred years, of handing on the burning torch. Now there was only Marcel left, and it was doubtful whether he would ever be well enough to take his place in the concern.

And at the very back of his mind there was something else, something he couldn't quite put a name to. It had been there, almost forgotten, frequently ignored, but draining his enthusiasm, slowing him down, pulling him back, ever since Angus's visit just before war broke out.

This elusive something could best be described as a tendency to question the values by which he had lived since marrying Claudine and settling down in Toulouse. At that time it had seemed to him that wealth, social position and success in business, were a worthy aim in life. It wasn't till Angus had turned up, bruised and battered and looking like a tramp, that the first crack appeared in Tim's armour of complacency. And when he had voiced his first faint doubts about his set of values, Angus had spoken of a missing element in Tim's life and in his own as well. And that had really disconcerted Tim.

During the first year of the war he heard occasionally from Angus in Paris. He would have liked to be given some sort of clue as to what that missing element was, but Angus never returned to the subject. Perhaps because he himself was equally uncertain about the whole matter. And then, after the Pétain government took over, Angus stopped writing. From then on Tim had been left to try and sort the puzzle out unaided, and had failed completely.

As one disaster after another struck the family Tim was left with no firm conviction about anything at all to sustain him. The first of the calamities, Gaston's death, had served to draw him and Claudine closer together in their grief. But when Monique ran away with Marco, husband and wife reacted in a less united manner. They both felt grief and shock, but in Claudine the dominating emotions were anger and outrage. Her chief concern seemed to be the knowledge that this action on the girl's part exposed them to the disgrace of having such totally discreditable connexions. They were now to suffer the contempt of all the good families of Toulouse. The best they could hope for was pity. Pity! The thought of it filled poor Claudine with impotent rage. That they, the Rougons, should be exposed to the pity of all their dearest friends and rivals was more than she could bear.

And so Monique and her unpresentable young man were consigned to utter oblivion. They were sacrificed to *les convenances*, in the hope that this total rupture would be seen to be sufficient amends for having such unacceptable connexions.

Keeping his place on the top rung of the social ladder had

never been one of Tim's main priorities. He enjoyed being there, and would have agreed that the privilege was worth a certain amount of sacrifice. But not the sacrifice of his daughter. After a series of fierce arguments Tim's resistance crumbled. Monique was never again to be mentioned, either within the family or without. But Tim made inquiries, found out where she was living with her regrettable husband, and went to see her. After that, he maintained regular though discreet contacts with her.

Claudine suspected that something of the sort was going on, but decided to leave well alone. Her chief concern was that no-one should know about the connexion. In a way she was even glad to think that Tim was still in touch with the errant daughter, for whom she grieved in much the same way as she grieved for her dead son. If Monique and Tim could find some comfort in each other's company, so much the better, provided the whole affair was kept secret. But she felt that her exalted position in the social hierarchy made it impossible for her to do more than turn a blind eye to the husband's continued relationship with the daughter. After all, turning a blind eye was part of a woman's lot in life, and she could name a few among her most elevated connexions who had been known to have to do this on more than one occasion, if in perhaps slightly different circumstances. Which husband, after all, was the guiltier, the one who sneaked off to meet his mistress, or this one, who refused to withdraw his love from a forbidden daughter?

The argument about the letters was left unresolved. Tim couldn't summon up enough courage to tell his wife that he didn't want to write the letters because he simply didn't want all that extra business. That, he knew, would have been heresy of the most despicable kind. So he continued his putting-off tactics in the hope that, if the letters were not written soon it would turn out to be too late to do anything. Too late is too late, and even Claudine would have to accept that unpalatable truth.

When Tim told her the following day that he would not be home for lunch Claudine assumed he was going to see Monique. She was about to inform their only remaining servant that her master would not require any lunch, when the idea came to her. She walked into the dining room and stood again at the window, stroking the frayed curtain. She looked at the dust on the furniture, the flaking paintwork, and thought, I'm going to put all this right. She stood entranced, seeing the room rise up before her in all its old splendour. She hesitated between renewing the old colour scheme or embarking on something new. It was a difficult choice. The room really had been superb as it was. On the other hand, colour was immensely important to Claudine, and it seemed a pity to lose the opportunity of trying out some new combination. After a few minutes of delicious indecision she began to consider whether perhaps she was being just a little previous. She had had her brilliant idea, true enough; but it still had to be put into practice, it still had to succeed. And however successful it might turn out to be, it would be months, perhaps years, before the wealth came flowing in as before. She would then have time enough to think about colour schemes.

Meanwhile, she must act.

She spent the rest of the morning making plans. If Tim was going to see Monique, that meant that he wouldn't be in the office till late afternoon. This left her ample time to put her plan into operation – unless, of course, old Dupont raised any difficulties. She was sure she could overcome any scruples he might have, but it might take time. So she had better go immediately after the lunch break.

Early in the afternoon she appeared at the office and was greeted with polite consternation.

Ah, *madame, monsieur* would not be back till much later. They were desolated! Claudine did her best to look disconcerted. Then she appeared to come to a decision. Well then, perhaps M. Dupont would be able to help her. Certainly, madame. M. Dupont was sent for and appeared, all bows.

Perhaps they could speak in her husband's office, she suggested.

When she explained her plan to her father's old secretary, M. Dupont was evidently flabbergasted.

'But *madame*, but *madame*,' was all he could say.

'Yes, M. Dupont, it's the only thing to do. Otherwise it will be too late.'

'So *madame* wishes me to write to all these former customers, in the name of . . . ?'

'Of the firm. Make sure my father's name appears. Don't you have any of the old headed paper, from before his death?'

'Yes, *madame*, but . . . these letters . . . they are to be signed by . . . ?'

'By me. I shall sign Claudine Baker Rougon. There's no problem about that. They will assume that my father's place has been taken over by his daughter. A perfectly reasonable supposition.'

'Certainly, perfectly reasonable. But . . . '

'But what, M. Dupont?'

The old man looked intensely uncomfortable:

'What about . . . M. Baker? Why does he not sign the letters?'

'Because he won't write them. I don't know why, but he refuses to write them. You can see for yourself how disastrous the results will be if these letters aren't written. We must make some effort to recapture this market. You see, don't you, how necessary this is?'

M. Dupont had no difficulty in agreeing with her. His whole working life had been spent in the firm, and he would have given anything to see it rise like a phoenix from its ashes. But the head was now M. Baker. Dupont's loyalties, in the event of a rupture, would certainly have been to the daughter of the Rougons. But the law, unfortunately, would side with the titular head. It was perhaps not the first time that Dupont had been forced to make a difficult decision in the interests of the firm. So far there had been no serious problems, and if old M. Rougon had occasionally sailed a little near the wind, at least on those occasions Dupont had known that he was acting on the instructions of his legal superior. This time he was being asked to defy the wishes of his employer, and that was a very different matter. With all the delicacy and diplomacy of an elderly Frenchman, Dupont managed to insinuate his fears into Claudine's consciousness.

'You have nothing to fear, M. Dupont. You are one of our oldest and most valued associates. I would never ask you to do anything for which I could not be personally answerable. I can assure you that I take full responsibility for what I am asking you to do. Should the question arise, I shall explain to my husband that I had some difficulty in persuading you. I can assure you that, whatever happens, you shall not be penalized.'

M. Dupont still appeared to hesitate.

'I appeal to you, *monsieur*, as to our oldest and most valued member of staff. It is for the sake of the firm. I know you share with me an undying loyalty to the family business, a loyalty that no outsider can be expected to understand.'

That appeal did the trick. This woman realized that his involvement with the firm was deeper and went back further than that of its present head. A spark of Gallic fire appeared in his old eyes.

'*Madame*,' he said, 'we shall save the firm, you and I, cost what it may. And now, *à l'oeuvre!*'

Long before there was any likelihood of Tim's return a batch of letters had been written and signed. Claudine took them with her and posted them right away. Dupont was to keep the rest of the staff away from Tim, just in case they mentioned her visit and he suspected that she'd been up to something. Never before had she been closeted with a member of the office staff, and the others must be wondering. But by tomorrow it wouldn't matter if Tim found out. The letters would be safely out of Rouen. No intervention on his part, in even the highest places, could stop them then.

The first step towards the restoration of the fallen fortunes of their firm had been taken.

When she came home from her shopping the following morning she saw Tim's car in the drive, long before the normal time, and braced herself for the interview. She hated having to go to market, but with only one servant there were days when the maid was too busy with other duties, and Claudine had to pocket her pride and do the shopping. She was always in a bad temper when she came back. As soon as she got into the hall she called the maid and handed her the two baskets. Then she walked into the little study, where she knew Tim would be waiting for her. It was an unwritten law of the household that serious conversations of her choosing took place in the dining room, and in Tim's study when he was the instigator.

'Well?' she said as she walked in. Her voice sounded as truculent as she felt. She was glad the interview was to take place now, with all her bad temper from the shopping to support her.

'So you've terrorized poor old Dupont into acting without my instructions?'

'I did not terrorize him. Poor old Dupont was only too glad to help save the firm. It matters more to him than anything else. Did he say I terrorized him?'

'Not in so many words. But he was very upset, and kept on insisting that he couldn't go against the wishes of your father's daughter. You bullied him into it.'

'If that's the impression he gave you, he's nothing but a treacherous old liar. He was only too glad to help.'

Both of them knew that they were arguing about a minor point, meanwhile rallying their forces for the battle to come.

'Who told you?' she asked.

'Dupont himself. He was most distressed about the whole thing.'

'Distressed? He was positively exultant. The old fox is trying to keep in with both of us. I see he has no need of my protection.'

Eventually they got on to the real issue. He wanted to know why she had written the letters and she wanted to know why he hadn't. In the end he confessed to his reluctance:

'I just don't see how we can cope with work on that scale any longer. It was different when your father was here. And if it hadn't been for the war we'd have had Gaston working with us by now. And Marcel, if his health permitted. I can't manage it all on my own.'

'But you wouldn't have to manage it all on your own. As business improves, you take on more staff. I'm surprised that even *you* haven't managed to grasp such an elementary concept.'

Tim was still reluctant to concede the feasibility of a

greater turnover of business. 'Besides . . . ' he said, and then remained silent.

'Besides what?'

'Well, I've been wondering over the past few years whether it's worth all the effort.'

He found Claudine's uncomprehending stare fixed on him. 'Not worth the effort? What on earth do you mean?'

Tim realized that the concept he was trying to explain to her was foreign to all her beliefs and experience, and he gave up in discouragement.

Claudine's exasperation broke forth. 'I just don't know what's the matter with you. You've lost your sense of values, your impetus, your . . . your everything. It's as if you were only half-alive. And it all goes back to the beginning of the war. I noticed it then, and it's gone on ever since. But I really thought that, now the war's over . . . '

'It's got nothing to do with the war.'

'Well, it coincided exactly with the beginning of the war. I spotted it at once.'

'It goes back further. Just a few days further.'

'To what?'

'To that day Angus appeared.'

'Looking like a tramp. Don't I remember! And what's his visit got to do with your deplorable attitude since then?'

'Well, it made me think about values.'

'Values?'

'Yes. Priorities. What's important and what isn't.'

'You mean you were sorry you hadn't gone off to Spain to fight for the Reds? If that's what you wanted, you had your chance here, you know. You could have joined the Resistance and enjoyed fighting the invader. There was nothing to stop you.'

'You would have been the first to stop me.'

Claudine realized she had made a tactical error here. During the years of the occupation, the Baker family had trod the delicate path of total non-commitment with regard to their feelings about the Germans. And even if Tim or any other member of the family had wished to declare against the invader, Claudine would have been the first to silence him.

The discussion ended with nothing settled. Tim wanted to make it absolutely clear that he was not prepared to handle a greater turnover of business; Claudine wanted to make it clear that this was utterly essential. It ended with each party more convinced than ever of the unshakeable rightness of his or her position. A sullen truce reigned over the house for the next few days.

It was ended, not to say shattered, by the arrival of an unexpected visitor. Claudine was crossing the hall one evening when she heard the front-door bell ring. She opened the door, looked at the figure standing outside and exclaimed, '*Ah, mon Dieu!*' She left Angus standing in the doorway and looked into the study where Tim was reading. '*C'est ton ami,*' she announced, with considerable emphasis on the possessive pronoun.

15

When the war was over, Angus found himself once again at a loose end. It seemed to be his normal state, periodically, at least. Where was he to go? What was he to do? He seemed to be running short of wars. What was left? The last time he had been in this position the obvious thing to do was go to Paris and resume his teaching life there. Now, he couldn't bear the thought of Paris. It would be too full of Marie's ghost. And the same applied to Rouen. That was what had driven him out of the place after her death.

Thinking of all the loose ends in his life, it occurred to him that he could perhaps do something towards tying some of them up. He would have dearly loved to go back to Catalonia to see Gil and Marta and the beautiful, mindless Quimeta. But that was out of the question. Six years after the end of the Civil War it was clear that Franco was not prepared to let bygones be bygones. In the first place, Angus knew that he would never be allowed into the country. The only way would be to get in as he had got out, walking over the mountains. But not through the Devil's Gorge this time, he thought with a shiver. And anyway, even if he got in and found his way to the *masia*, his presence would certainly prove compromising for his friends. No, it looked as if it would be many years before he could even think of going back.

He would also have liked to go and see his two captors, the Civil Guards, and find out what really lay behind the superb piece of inefficiency that had allowed him to escape. That particular pipe-dream, however, he abandoned with less reluctance. But he felt so deeply moved by all that Gil and Marta had done for him, by all they had risked for his sake, that it still seemed to him a cruel quirk of fate that he could find no way of getting in touch with them, of letting them know how much he valued them.

He also wanted to go back and see his shepherd again. That at least ought to be feasible. And there were Tim and Claudine. He couldn't quite make up his mind whether he wanted to see them again, or whether they were likely to want to see him. He was pretty sure Claudine wouldn't. But Tim was an old friend. It was perhaps worth making an effort to renew the relationship. The least he could do was turn up and explain why he had stopped writing. Tim would surely understand once he knew the circumstances in which Angus was placed in Rouen.

There was another visit he wanted to make in Toulouse, to his old friend Pierre, though he felt some misgivings about this one. The trouble was that Pierre was married to Marie's sister, and he felt he might not yet be strong enough to face this encounter.

He boarded the train for Toulouse without having come to any decision as to whether he would go and see Pierre and Annette. Then he told himself that it would be ridiculous not to go if he was in Toulouse anyway. Besides, he thought, if I see them I can then go and take first-hand news of them to the Merciers. For he had decided that, painful as it would be for him to revisit the house in which he had spent years beside

Marie, he simply could not fail to go back and see the parents. It would be monstrous not to go.

When he got off the train in Toulouse he still had the final decision to make. Would he go and see the Bakers first, or would he leave that till after he had made the more difficult contact? Suddenly he remembered the consternation that his bedraggled appearance had caused in their elegant home, and he decided with a rueful smile that he couldn't possibly turn up again looking little better than he had the last time. That settled it. He would go straight to Pierre and Annette's house. There at least he felt sure they would approve of the reason for his dishevelled appearance.

As he rang the bell it occurred to him that it might have been better to let them know beforehand that he was coming. But his recent experiences had made all the normal forms recede into the background. It probably wouldn't matter that much.

Pierre's reception of him made it clear that it didn't matter at all. He was overjoyed to see his old friend, and called Annette at once.

But it was a difficult meeting.

The ghost of Marie seemed to be hovering very near as Angus met her sister for the first time and Annette met her sister's lover. Looking at Annette, Angus realized the truth of what Mme Mercier had said about the two girls. She had compared them to candles. Annette, she had said, 'sheds a sweet and gentle light. Her flame does not burn so bright, but it will last longer.' Time had proved her right about the speed with which Marie's candle was to burn out. Now, seeing Annette, he realized that she had also been right about the sweet and gentle light.

Within minutes of arriving in the house Angus was feeling completely at home, and very glad that he had come. They had a great deal to tell each other about the missing years in their lives. It appeared that his hosts had also been deeply involved in the Resistance, though less spectacularly than Marie.

They spoke a great deal about her. Angus had always found it hard to believe that she had been the younger of the two sisters, and Annette agreed that this did seem a bit surprising. 'She was two years younger than me, but she was always the leader. Even when we were tiny little things. When I was four and she was only two, it was Marie who had all the ideas. And if I ever happened to have one of my own, it was still Marie who took the lead.'

'And you didn't mind?'

'No, I really don't think I minded. She had so much charm. And she carried such conviction, even then.'

'Yes, charm and conviction, that's just about it. That was Marie.'

Annette's eyes had clouded with tears. 'It's bad enough for the rest of us,' she said. 'I don't know how you can bear it.'

Angus sat silent for a moment. Then he said, 'One has to bear it.'

'And life goes on,' put in Pierre. 'What are your plans for the future?'

'I wish I knew. I have no long-term plans.'

'But now, in the short term?'

'I want to see one or two people here in the south. People who helped me. And then I want to go back to Rouen and see your parents, Annette.'

'They will be so happy to see you. I know how much they thought of you.'

'And then I'll go back to England and look up the parents of two of my comrades in the Spanish Civil War. And after that I just don't know.'

'Go home to your own people, perhaps?' suggested Pierre.

'Perhaps. But I haven't thought that far ahead yet.'

'You are not happy with your people?' asked Annette.

Angus shook his head. 'No, not very.'

'That is sad.' The words were uttered very sweetly and softly, but Angus wondered whether perhaps there was a gentle touch of reproach in among the regret .

'That's something I want to think about. Going back, I mean.'

Annette smiled. 'Well, I'm glad you're at least prepared to think about it.'

Before going to bed, Angus turned to Annette with a question that had just struck him. 'Did Marie know that you were involved in the Resistance?'

'No. It wasn't the sort of thing one dared put on paper. And we had no personal contact during all those years. We didn't know that *she* was – or rather, no one had told us. But we knew, didn't we, Pierre?'

'Yes. We knew Marie. The rest followed inevitably. Can you imagine her sitting back and doing nothing?'

'Never. Never,' Suddenly Angus realized that he had no idea what Marie would have been like in peacetime. Would she have been bored? Would she have felt that her life was futile? If she had been a man he felt sure that she would have gone off somewhere to fight someone else's war for them. More or less what he had done, but out of conviction and a sense of adventure. Once again he began to wonder what exactly he *had* been doing in the last two wars. He had joined in the Spanish Civil War out of pique, and in this last one out of blind obedience to Marie's ideals.

The only war he had fought for any genuine reason had been the First World War. He had fought that one with all the idealism of youth. Or so he had thought at the time. Looking back now he felt that his enthusiasm had stemmed just as much from a desire not to be left out, a burning anxiety to show how grown-up and competent he was. Fighting in the trenches had been the first occasion on which he had felt he was on a level with Gavin. The only occasion, really.

After a few days his hosts had got him sufficiently respectable-looking for him to feel he could approach the Bakers. This time at least they wouldn't have to smuggle him upstairs and into a bath and a set of Tim's clothes before they deemed him fit for the servants to see. This time, he felt, he ought to get a less strained reception.

When he got to the villa he was astonished to see the state of decay that the garden was in. And, standing in the porch as he rang the bell, he saw that the house seemed to be doing no better. He remembered the fears that the couple had expressed about the prospects for their business in the event of a war. He hadn't really paid much attention at the time, convinced that the members of the business world always knew how to look after themselves. This time it certainly looked as if he had been wrong.

When Claudine opened the door and left him standing he realized he had been wrong again about his reception. Instead of being better it was manifestly worse. He was just wondering whether to go away again when Tim appeared.

Once again Angus's expectations were proved wrong. Tim greeted him with a warmth and eagerness that quite took him by surprise. Tim apologized for Claudine's rudeness and explained that things were just a little difficult at the moment.

'You see what the war has done to us,' he said, with a gesture that took in the whole of their dilapidated surroundings. Angus was dismayed to see what the house was like. This time, it seemed, his appearance and that of the house were mismatched once again, but in the opposite direction. I never seem to get it right, he thought, as he viewed Tim's distinctly shabby smoking jacket.

As they exchanged news they learned of the loss and suffering that the war had brought to each, and soon felt closer to each other than at any point during Angus's previous visit.

During all this time Claudine had stayed away, refusing to welcome the unwelcome guest. Tim was uncomfortably aware of this, and felt he ought to offer some explanation. But it was difficult to do this without letting Angus see how things stood between himself and his wife. There was also the problem of Claudine's conviction that Angus was to blame for much of what was wrong with their lives. However, as time went by, and an explanation became increasingly unavoidable, he suddenly saw that this would be a good opportunity to broach the subject that had been worrying him for so long. Haltingly, he gave his explanation.

'The point is', he went on, 'that Claudine is convinced it's thanks to you that I'm not taking as active a part in the affairs of the firm as she would like.'

'Really? What on earth's it got to do with me?'

'Well, do you remember that last day, when I drove you to the station? Remember I said something – oh, I can't remember how I put it, but something to the effect that your visit with its account of all your adventures had left me feeling as if I'd missed out on something?'

'Yes, vaguely.'

'And you spoke of the missing element in my life. And then you disconcerted me by suggesting there was a missing element in your life too. Remember?'

'Yes. I think I mentioned that shepherd. He seemed to me the ideal of the happy man.'

'Well, ever since then I've kept on asking myself whether

we'd really got the right set of values, Claudine and I and all our wealthy and successful friends. I could never come up with the answer. But the doubt kept niggling at me, and it sapped my sense of purpose and my enterprise. And now, now we have a really big problem on our hands.'

He explained about the battle that was raging between him and his wife about the extent to which the business should be encouraged to grow in the new postwar climate, and of his reluctance to get involved once again in the treadmill of business success and the social round. Especially now that none of the children was with them. What was the point?

When it came to the bit about Claudine's intervention in the affair of the letters Angus was tempted to show his admiration.

'That was quite an enterprising thing to do,' he remarked.

'I suppose it was,' conceded Tim. 'Rather too enterprising for my liking.'

'Still, don't you think she's got something there? She's a pretty intelligent woman, isn't she?'

'Oh yes, she's intelligent enough. That's why I never win any of the arguments. You're not going to take her side, are you?'

'No, certainly not. But she's just given me an idea. As you know, I'm not much good at solving my own problems, or at solving other people's, for that matter. But I've just had an idea that might solve yours.'

The idea, he explained, was that Claudine should be encouraged to take a more active part in the business. That would take some of the burden off Tim's shoulders, while yet allowing for the expansion that she considered so necessary.

'In other words,' said Tim, 'if she wants the profits she can do some of the work. Sounds reasonable enough.'

'Would she take it on, do you think?'

'She might. She just might. She has a lot of energy, and perhaps it's looking for an outlet.'

A few days later a reply came from one of the firms Claudine had written to. It enclosed a gratifyingly large order. Tim followed the plan that he and Angus had worked out. He brought the letter home and handed it over to Claudine.

She was delighted when she saw it. 'There you are,' she exclaimed as soon as she had read it. 'Didn't I tell you?'

'Yes, my dear, you were perfectly right. Perhaps you would care to deal with it yourself?'

'Me? It's got nothing to do with me.'

'But it has. It was you who wrote the letter. I think you should deal with the order.'

'Don't be ridiculous.'

'Well then, shall I just throw the letter away? I'm not going to deal with it. It has nothing to do with me.'

'But I can't deal with it. It's not my job.'

'You can make it your job. You'll get all the co-operation you need from the rest of the staff. Especially Dupont.'

'But I don't know anything about it.'

'You've just proved that you do. And anyway, you're your father's daughter. You seem to have inherited his talent. You should use it.'

Claudine was about to advance another argument against Tim's suggestion, but suddenly she stopped herself. Slowly, she picked up the letter and read its contents again.

The following day Tim handed his wife two more letters, both with orders included. This was what Claudine had been waiting for. She was not prepared to intervene in the business for one order only. But if her hunch had proved right, and business was indeed looking up as a result of her action, then it would be worth her while to take a hand in it.

'When are you going to see Monique next?' she asked.

Tim looked up, startled. Nothing had ever been said of his secret visits to their daughter. 'Tomorrow,' he said, in a strained voice.

'Well then, will you tell Dupont that I'll have some matters to settle with him in the afternoon? I should like the use of your room.'

'Certainly, my dear.' She hadn't exactly asked him for the use of his room, but he felt that the fact that she'd even mentioned it was a step in the right direction.

The following morning, as he was leaving the house, Claudine said, 'You can tell her . . . tell her I hope she's well.'

Angus was leaving Toulouse the following day, and the two friends met in a café for a last chat. They both felt this would be pleasanter than meeting in Tim's house with a hostile Claudine in the background.

Angus was delighted to hear that Claudine had made the decision they were hoping for.

'So she's going to take charge of all that part of the business?' he asked.

'So it seems. I stick to my usual routine, and she takes charge of all the business she herself has generated. And I suspect that, once she gets a taste for it, she'll generate a whole lot more.'

He then told Angus about the slightly mellower mood in which she seemed to be, to the extent of acknowledging her daughter's existence and sending her a message. They tried to discover what exactly it was that had caused this change, and decided it must be a combination of having found something positive to do with her energies, her pleasure at being able to continue in the family firm where her father had left off, and the prospect of a renewal of their more prosperous days.

'Come to think of it, life must have been rather bloody for her for a long time, given her values,' said Angus.

'I suppose you're right. But it's awfully decent of you to see it this way, considering how she behaves to you.'

'Well, I can't expect every woman to fall for my fatal charm. And if she thinks I was instrumental in leading you astray from the true path of success in business, she's got a lot to forgive me for.'

'One of these days I'm going to tell her it was you who thought of getting her involved. But I think it's a bit soon just yet.'

'Far too soon. You don't want to put her off at this stage. Better to wait till she's thoroughly hooked on money-making. I gather it's quite addictive.'

'It certainly is. Especially for the first twenty years or so. After that it loses some of its glamour. It has for me, at any rate.'

'Perhaps that's what I ought to try. If I could stick to the same thing — no matter what — for twenty years, I'd be doing remarkably well.'

Tim laughed. 'You wouldn't stick it for ten days. It's far too dull.'

'Dull? Making all that lovely money?'

'You have to distinguish between having it and making it. And the making bit comes first, and that's the dull bit. It's the having it that's addictive.'

'I hope Claudine doesn't find the making bit so dull that she gives up.'

'She won't find it dull, not her. It runs in the blood in that family.' After a pause Tim said, 'Seriously, though, have you thought at all about what you're going to do with your life?'

'Seriously, I've thought and thought. But I just can't seem to come up with anything I'd like to do.'

'That's the problem, isn't it?'

'What do you mean?'

'The problem is that you're only prepared to consider doing what you would *like* to do.'

'And what's wrong with that?'

'Nothing. Only it narrows the choice.'

Angus sat in silence, looking thoughtful.

After a while, Tim said:

'Have you never done anything you really didn't want to do?'

'Yes, once. I went back to Kintalloch to help the family out when my father wasn't able to cope.'

'And you hated it?'

'No, actually, I found I liked it.'

'Then why didn't you stay on?'

'I did something stupid. I got myself involved with my sister-in-law. In the end I realized that the only decent thing I could do was to clear out.'

'So you can't go back?'

'Because of that? Oh, that's all right now. That was about twenty years ago. But there are other problems. You know what families are.' Angus had never told Tim about his confrontation with his son. What was the point of going into all that?

'It's a pity,' was Tim's comment. 'That might really be the place for you.'

This time it was Angus who was left with the feeling that his friend had given him something to think over. Not that he could go back to Kintalloch, that was clear. But the idea of perhaps doing something that didn't particularly appeal to him . . . this certainly opened up new horizons. After all, the only time he'd ever done anything of the sort had been when he went back to Kintalloch and found that he really enjoyed the life there, and felt he belonged. If only he hadn't spoilt it all by getting involved with Meg!

That afternoon Claudine spent some time with old Dupont. They both emerged from Tim's office looking remarkably pleased with life. Old Dupont felt that at last the business was going to be saved; Claudine shared this happy conviction, and, in addition, felt elated at the thought that it was she who was saving it.

In the evening she was feeling sufficiently benign to ask Tim whether he'd conveyed her message to their daughter.

'Yes, yes. I told her.' Tim sounded noncommittal.

'Well, what did she say?'

'Nothing much, really.' In fact Monique had said a great deal, but Tim felt that nothing could be gained by repeating it.

Claudine was hurt. It was obvious that the girl had not responded positively to her olive branch.

Had she reacted as a dutiful and repentant daughter should, her mother might have gone a step further. But Tim judged that Claudine was certainly not ready to accept the response of a defiant, wilful daughter who was still trying to come to terms with the results of her imprudent marriage. It would take a lot of time and patience before both parties could find a halfway spot where they could even think of meeting. Tim thought again of Angus's words:

'You know what families are.'

Yes, indeed, he thought, don't I just know!

16

Angus left Annette and Pierre with the promise that he would go back and see them on his way to Rouen after he had paid his visit to the shepherd. He meditated on the difference between the two couples he had been in contact with since arriving in Toulouse. It was clear that Tim and Claudine had a lot of problems to sort out, whereas Annette and Pierre seemed to be remarkably happy together. He wondered whether it was just because they were so much younger, but didn't very much like to think that this could be the explanation. After all, he and Tim were the same age, and he was not prepared to accept that this necessarily meant they had passed the age when happiness could be expected.

Perhaps it was simply that Tim and Claudine seemed to be mismatched, whereas the other two seemed made for each other. Like Marie and me, he thought. And then he began to wonder whether the success of these two relationships should perhaps be attributed to the girls. Annette was not at all like Marie in anything superficial – appearance, temperament, abilities. But they both had something in common which he found it hard to put a finger on. Perhaps it was simply a matter of excellence. Each was a perfect example of her type.

Now that he had parted from his friends, his sense of loss

and despair over Marie's death returned to him. He felt that nothing could ever wipe this out or lessen the intensity of his grief. It was all very well for them to talk about what he was going to do with his life. He had no life without Marie, that's what it came to.

He was still in an intensely gloomy and self-pitying mood when he got to the little village in the Pyrenees. He made inquiries and learned that, yes, Alphonse was *là-haut* with his flock, so he set off immediately for the hut. It was mid afternoon when he got there, and there was no sign of the shepherd. Angus knew he must still be on the higher pastures, and went to meet him as he came down with his flock, just as he had done during the days he had spent at the hut.

As he walked and looked at the green slopes about him he felt his gloom gradually lifting. Was it just the prospect of seeing Alphonse, or did the joyous green all about him contribute to the sense of emotional wellbeing? Soon he heard the thin, pure, familiar sound of the shepherd's pipe coming from behind the hillock ahead of him. The sound stopped and the figure came into view, outlined against the sky.

Angus waved, and Alphonse waved back. But instead of coming to meet him, as Angus expected, the shepherd stopped and put his pipe to his lips again. He was playing the Spanish folk song that Angus had taught him. By the time he had played the melody through twice, Angus had got to within speaking distance.

'You must teach me some more of these songs,' said the shepherd in a conversational tone, as if they had only been parted a few minutes. 'That one is so beautiful. Do you know any more like it?'

Angus had stopped, slightly taken aback at this matter-of-fact reception. The shepherd laughed, stepped forward to cover the distance between them, and embraced Angus. 'I knew you'd come back,' he said. 'I never doubted it, war or no war. But it's been a long time.'

'Six years,' said Angus. 'Too long. Far too long.'

'Yes, too long. But, *que voulez-vous?* People do these idiotic things. They must have their wars. *C'est trop bête.* I suppose you were mixed up in this one too, *n'est-ce pas?*'

Angus confessed that he had been. 'But at least I was on the right side,' he added in self-vindication.

'One always is, *mon cher*, one always is. Even the Germans, they knew they were on the right side.' Seeing Angus's crestfallen appearance the old man added, 'But then, it's easy for me to moralize. I'm too old to be caught up in it. And up here, in these mountains . . . in these blessed mountains,' he added, smiling at the austere landscape about him, 'these things don't really touch us. The air is too pure here for such evil things.'

'Except, perhaps, in the Devil's Gorge?'

'True, true,' conceded the shepherd. 'But then, as I explained, that is by special dispensation. You remember the story I told you?'

'Of course I remember it. I hope you have more stories like it to tell.'

'When the moment comes.'

'And I shall teach you more songs – when the moment comes.'

The shepherd looked at him with a twinkle in his eyes and then burst out laughing. 'Well, I'm glad to see you've survived the war. War can kill more things than flesh and blood.'

'Perhaps,' agreed Angus, 'but nothing else is so important. When you kill the flesh and blood you kill everything else as well.'

The old man caught the bitterness in his voice. 'I see you have a great sorrow,' he said.

They walked down to the hut in silence.

By the following day they had adopted their old routine. The shepherd set off in the morning and Angus went to meet him in the late afternoon. Then they walked back down to the hut together.

This time Angus didn't have the need to rest and recover from his injuries as on the previous occasion. But the long hours of silence and idleness were as necessary to him as the extra sleep had been the first time. The sheer, uncluttered size of the landscape was healing in itself. Angus felt as if for years he had had too many things crowded in on him, crowded into too small a space. It was perhaps the aftereffects of the years of captivity in Rouen – happy captivity, with Marie's presence, but a constricting experience all the same.

He now felt as if he were a tightly tangled skein of yarn which was being gently teased out, its knots gradually loosening. He had imagined he would tell the shepherd all about Marie and his sorrow over her death, but it wasn't necessary. The man knew, even though he had been given none of the details. He seemed to understand that what Angus needed most at that moment was silence, a rest from speech, his own as well as that of others. Gradually the clutter of thoughts in Angus's mind began to clear. He spent a lot of time lying on the grass, staring up at the sky; not thinking, hardly even feeling.

By the time late afternoon came and he went up the hill to meet the shepherd he was ready for conversation, of a gentle, chatting variety. No more discussion of problems. He felt he was on holiday from problems – his own and other people's as well. Vaguely, he wondered how Tim and Claudine were getting on. It would be nice to find out, some time, that things were going better for them. But just at this moment there was no urgency about it. No urgency about his own problems either. For the moment none of these things mattered. The sky mattered, the green of the grass, the clear, sharp, unambiguous outline of the mountains mattered.

In the evening Angus sang songs for the shepherd to memorize and play on his pipe. Alphonse was particularly fond of some of the old Hebridean melodies that Angus taught him, though he found them more difficult to learn.

'They are not so easy, these songs,' he would say. 'They make me work hard. But they are very beautiful.' Then he would add reflectively, 'I think they must be very complicated, your people. They have strange melodies.'

One evening Angus asked him whether the moment had not yet come.

'For a story? It's my turn now, *n'est-ce pas?* Well, we'll see if there's a story anywhere about.' He sat and thought in silence for a while before beginning his tale.

'Once upon a time,' he said, ' — is that the one you want?'

'The very one,' said Angus solemnly.

'Well, then. Once upon a time there was a tree, a beautiful willow tree. We don't get any of them up here, it's too high and too cold. But down, way down in the valleys you'll find them, and very beautiful they are. Well, this willow tree lived beside a stream, a bright, clear, chattering stream, so the willow always had plenty of water, and grew to be a tall, graceful tree. And, like so many trees, it passed its life in a sort of quiet, peaceful dream, letting the breeze blow through its leaves and leaning over the stream to keep the water cool with its shadow. It could hear the chattering of the stream, but it never troubled to find out what it was saying. And then one day it woke up just enough to listen to what the stream kept on repeating. "I'm going to see the world, I'm going to see the world, don't stop me, anybody, I'm in such a hurry, I'm off to see the world." And the tree was filled with a great longing to go and see the world, just like the stream. "Wait for me," it cried, "I'm coming too. I want to see the world, just like you. Wait for me." "Can't wait, can't wait," sang the stream, "I'm in *such* a hurry. Can't wait for you, you're much too slow. Can't wait, can't wait for anybody. I'm faster than any of you, and I'm off to see the world."

'Well, the tree was rather upset, and decided it would go off and see the world on its own, without bothering about the stream. So it tried to lift one root, and then another, and then another. But nothing. It simply couldn't move. So it decided it would have to get the stream to help it. But again the stream refused. It even laughed scornfully and called the tree a stick-in-the-mud. Now, the tree thought this was rather unfair because, if there was any mud about, it was all of the stream's making. After all, no water, no mud. Stands to reason, thought the tree.

'But it was so anxious to go and see the world that it decided to overlook this little affront. So it begged the stream again, as earnestly as it knew how, to take it along on its journey. "Can't wait, can't wait," sang the stream, "I'm off to see the world." Then the tree leaned over as far as it could, trying to catch hold of the stream with its leaves. But the water flowed through them just as easily as the breeze blew through them, so the tree just couldn't get a grip. And the stream flowed past, laughing merrily. And the willow wept.

'And God happened to be out walking just there. For God is very fond of the green fields and the trees and the streams, even foolish, wilful little streams like this one. And he heard the silvery laughter and went over to see what all the mirth was about. And he found the willow weeping, and asked it why it was so sad, and the willow told him. And God was very annoyed with the stream, and he called over one of the clouds that usually hang about the mountain tops, and he told it to be sure not to let any rain fall on the nearby hills for a few weeks. "That'll show it. That'll teach it to go about laughing at one of my trees. But don't let it dry up altogether," he warned the cloud. "It's a very young stream, and I don't want to be too hard on it. But it has to learn its lesson. I can't have it behaving in this rude way." "That's right," said the cloud, "*Toujours la politesse.*"

'And then God turned to the tree to console it. "Now, tell me, why are you so anxious to go with the stream?" "Because I w-w-want to see the w-w-world," sobbed the willow. It took God all his time not to burst out laughing. But he knew how sensitive trees are, especially willows, and this one was obviously very upset to begin with. So he managed to keep a perfectly straight face and said, "You know, I think that silly little stream has got you all confused. No matter where it goes, it can't possibly see anything that *isn't* the world. And it can't possibly see any more world than you can see right here."

'"You mean . . . you mean . . . ?"

'"That's right. This *is* the world," said God solemnly. "And what's more, strictly *entre nous*, this is one of the very best bits of world I ever managed to create. And, needless to say, so are all the others," he added under his breath.

'And the tree looked round about it as it never had before. And it saw it all, really *saw* it all for the first time, and it could hardly believe the beauty of the world. And, being a willow, it wept again. But this time it wept for joy.'

After the shepherd had finished speaking Angus said, 'You're the tree, aren't you?'

Alphonse nodded. 'Yes, I've been a tree all my life.'

'And I'm the stream?'

The shepherd shrugged gently. 'What do *you* think?'

'Yes, I'm the stream, all right. Always rushing off somewhere else. No roots.'

'You have roots,' Alphonse said. Then he took his pipe out of his pocket and began softly playing some of the songs Angus had just taught him.

'Can the stream ever become a tree?' Angus asked in one of the pauses.

The shepherd considered his answer for a moment. 'Not in the story. That would confuse the listener, and you must never do that. You have to stick to the rules. But real life is different. It is longer, and slower – *ça évolue*. In real life, yes, it is possible. In real life practically everything is possible.'

17

By the time he left the shepherd's hut Angus felt pretty certain that he now wanted to go back to his roots, back to Kintalloch. For the first time he realized that sooner or later he was going to have to face the problem of his relationship with his son. He must go back, though he had no idea how to set about it. His people presumably thought him dead. He would have to find some way of preparing them for his return. He couldn't just turn up out of the blue and say, Here I am, not dead after all.

He was thinking of this as he sat in the train on his way back to Toulouse, when he suddenly remembered the episode in which Tartarin goes back to Tarascon and finds all his neighbours in the church, holding a funeral service for him. He was unable to hold back a burst of laughter at the thought of the dismay that a similar return from his presumed grave might produce among the good people of Kintalloch. His companions in the compartment looked at him in astonishment and alarm. He thought he'd better explain, and told them that he had just remembered the Tartarin episode. That immediately set their minds at rest. As good *méridionaux* they all knew and loved their Tartarin, and the rest of the journey was kept lively with similar reminiscences.

In Toulouse he went straight to Annette and Pierre's house. His plan was to spend a few days with them, see Tim, and then go on to Rouen to stay with the Merciers for a while. After that there would be the business of looking up Dick's parents and trying to find Bob's. Then he would be free to tackle the problem of how to present himself at Kintalloch.

When he got to the flat, however, he saw he would have to change his plans. Word had come from Rouen that M. Mercier was very ill. Cancer of the lung had been diagnosed, and the prognosis was not good. Annette had gone off at once to help her mother look after the invalid.

'It's really rather difficult,' said Pierre. 'You see, we've just discovered that Annette is pregnant, and she's not feeling at all well. She'd be much better here at home. But her mother needs help. What can one do?'

'I'll go,' said Angus, without pausing for thought. 'I was going there anyway, as you know. I'll just go sooner. And Annette can come back here. I'll stay as long as I can be of help.'

'But Angus, do you know what you're letting yourself in for? Have you ever nursed a sick person?'

'No, never. But I did look after my son a great deal when his mother was . . . indisposed, shall we say? I shouldn't think it will be all that different. And I can learn. I'm a good learner, you know, an excellent beginner. It's more or less what I've spent my life doing. Beginning again and again.'

It was decided that he would leave the following morning. Meanwhile he should have time for a quick visit to Tim's house, just to say goodbye.

He rang the bell and waited in the porch. The garden was still in the same state of abandon; but he noticed that a large earthenware pot had been placed in the porch, with a mixture of brightly coloured geraniums spilling out of it. He hoped this was symbolical.

When the door was opened he was disconcerted to find Claudine staring at him, and disappointed to hear that Tim was out.

'I just came to say goodbye. I'm leaving tomorrow, earlier than I thought. Will you tell him I'm sorry I missed him?'

Claudine looked at him in silence for a moment, then said: 'Come in.'

'Are you sure?'

'I am always sure. Come in.'

She led him into the dining room and asked him to sit down. Then they stared at each other for what seemed to Angus a very long time. He didn't know whether to expect polite conversation or a violent tirade.

Eventually Claudine broke the silence:

'Tim is taking Monique back to some barbarous village up in the hills where she lives with the Spanish good-for-nothing that she took it into her head to marry. It's a long way, and he won't be back for at least another two hours.'

'Monique has been here?'

'Yes. She has been here. It is the first time.' Claudine looked so austere that Angus didn't know whether to congratulate or commiserate with her.

'Are you glad?' he asked.

Claudine sat silent for a while, staring out of the window. Then she said, 'Yes, I am glad now. But it was horrible. She is very angry, very bitter.'

'I expect she too thinks she has a right to be angry,' Angus put in tentatively. Why is she telling me this, he wondered. Can it mean she is beginning to soften towards me? Or is it just that she feels she has to talk to someone about it, no matter who?

'Tim thinks I have been unreasonable about our daughter. What do you think?'

Angus was completely taken aback. The last thing he had expected was for this woman to value his opinion on any subject under the sun. He floundered for a moment. Then he managed to say, 'I think it's the sort of situation where it's almost impossible for anyone to be reasonable. But if you all try, and keep on trying . . . '

'Monique is not trying. Far from it. But I am trying, now, and Tim, poor Tim, he has been trying all along.'

'Well, that should do the trick. But it may take a long time.'

'Yes, it has been a long time already.'

Angus was so pleased that Claudine was talking to him that he decided to risk bringing up the matter of her intervention in the business.

'I understand you're taking a hand in running the business now?'

'Someone had to do something.'

That didn't sound very auspicious. Angus thought he'd better avoid any discussion of Tim's role in the firm.

'Are you enjoying it?' he asked guardedly.

Suddenly Claudine's face lit up:

'Yes, immensely. It is so interesting. Now I see why you men do all this type of thing and keep the women out. It is because they want it all for themselves. It is so much more interesting than the work they leave for the women. And if I hadn't taken the law into my own hands and intervened I'd never have known what I was missing. Nothing, but nothing of all that's left for the women to do is of any importance or of any interest. I go to market, yes? and I buy steak or I buy pork, right? And what on earth does it matter? Look!' she stood up energetically and walked over to the window. 'These curtains, see these curtains? A few weeks ago the most important thing in my life was to try and find a way of renewing them, with no money, *bien entendu*. But now I have other things to think about. Oh yes, the curtains will be renewed one day, and that will be very nice. But not important. Not transcendental, as it seemed a few weeks ago. I have something better to do now. But if I had not taken the law into my own hands, and insisted on action, then I'd still be sitting alone in this room, caressing my frayed curtains and watching the dust pile up on my furniture.'

'I see you are a woman of action. I'm glad you've found your vocation.'

Angus left soon after that, promising to write to Tim.

18

It was a strange feeling, arriving in Rouen, this city that he had lived in for several years and never seen. He had arrived with Marie when it was dark and been taken straight to her home, from which he had not emerged till he had left it, again at night, making for the outskirts of the town to avoid being seen. Marie was fond of her native city, and had often spoken to him about the beauty of its Gothic buildings. But that, of course, was before the bombs had done their work. He knew that the centre of the city must now be a sad sight.

He arrived at her home unannounced, and caused quite a stir. When he explained that he had come to take Annette's place the surprise was even greater. It took him some time to persuade them that he really meant it, and even then it was decided that Annette would stay on for a few days, just to make sure that the arrangement would work. Invalids can be difficult to handle, they pointed out. And M. Mercier, they had to confess, was by no means the easiest of invalids. A man who had reached the age of seventy with never a day's illness, and now . . . It was very hard. They had been told he could expect another six months, perhaps less.

It was well over a year since Angus had left Rouen, and he found both Merciers greatly changed. Marie's death had evidently taken its toll, and now there was this cancer business. An air of desolation seemed to hang over the whole family, Annette included. Even the joy of expecting her first child was dimmed by the family gloom. Angus thought that the sooner she got back to Toulouse the better, although the parents would miss her. He might be of material assistance, but he couldn't hope to be a substitute for her in the emotional sphere.

Why me, why me, why should this happen to *me?* That was the dominating thought in M. Mercier's mind, and it coloured every aspect of his present life. It was as if he simply couldn't get over the monstrous unfairness of the thing.

The sudden appearance of Angus startled him out of his self-pity.

'And you have come to help? That is wonderfully good of you. I am overwhelmed. And you can leave everything, you have no other commitments?'

Angus shook his head. 'That's the one advantage of leading my kind of errant life. No ties, so it means I'm available.'

M. Mercier nodded thoughtfully. 'Yes, yes. But it's very good of you all the same. I do appreciate it. The whole family, that is.'

'Your family looked after *me* for a long time,' pointed out Angus.

'Ah yes, yes. Those were difficult years. It was the least we could do. Nearly four years, wasn't it? This will not take nearly so long.' And he sighed. His gloom had descended on him once again.

Later on, when he was alone, the word 'available' that he had himself used, came back to Angus. He suddenly saw that, apart from the five years he had spent looking after Louis, and his periods of captivity in Rouen and in Spain, he had been available very nearly all his life. No commitments – or

138

at least none that could not be easily ended. His teaching, his translation, his relationships with most of the women in his life, none of these involved an inescapable obligation. Even his more heroic commitments in the Spanish Civil War and in the Resistance, all these were by definition temporary. We've got past the stage of the Hundred Years' War, he thought. No modern war could go on that long. In this day and age, war is strictly temporary. With a shock he realized that even his experience of fatherhood had been temporary; had, indeed, been intended to be so. From the start Louis was to be handed over to Kintalloch.

That was his son's *raison d'être*. Perhaps, he thought, perhaps it's time I put my availability to some more permanent use. He would have time to think it over during the next few months.

After the trial period it was unanimously agreed that he would make a very good nurse cum housekeeper, and Annette was sent off to Toulouse again, with the promise that they would send for her if things became too difficult.

His illness and the resentment with which he endured it brought out the martinet in M. Mercier. His wife confessed to Angus that during the early years of their marriage he had been quite a domestic tyrant, with all the traditional Frenchman's conviction of his own superiority and the right that this gave him to absolute authority.

'I suffered, oh yes, I suffered a great deal at first. But I had married him because of his wit and his charm and his intelligence, and the *je ne sais quoi* that goes into making an attractive personality, and all that was still there. So I bore his outbursts and his domination, and in the end he became mellower and gentler. Even in the face of great difficulties, even under the sorrow of Marie's death, he was wonderful. A reformed character. And now this! Believe me, seeing him react like this to his illness is almost as bad as knowing how ill he is, and that he is going to die. I feel as if I had already lost my husband.'

Angus did his best to comfort her. 'Perhaps he'll adjust. It must be a terrible shock to be told you're dying. And to feel so ill. Especially if you've been well and strong all your life. He's had no preparation for this sort of thing. Perhaps he'll adjust in time. After all, look at how well you've adjusted, and it must have been just as much of a shock to you.'

'It was a shock, yes, I own it. Almost as bad as Marie's death. And coming so soon after! But yet . . . he is my husband, and I have loved him and shared his life for over forty years, and I would give my life for him − at least, I think I would − but yet, it is not I who have to die, and perhaps that makes all the difference. Perhaps I would react with the same bitterness if I knew it was me who was going to die. All of us, we are separate, however close we may be. It's not me, it's him who is dying, and perhaps that's all that matters. I might react in the same way. And besides, he's the one who has to endure the pain and the illness. All the physical suffering is his.'

Angus stuck to his guns. 'Yes, I know, all this is true. But the fact remains that you've had a terrible shock to endure, and yet it hasn't rocked you off balance. If the shock has been even greater for him, that's all the more reason for thinking that he'll need more time to adjust.'

Mme Mercier laid her hand briefly on Angus's. 'Always,' she said, 'for the rest of your life, if you are unhappy, if you feel you have not achieved as much as you would like to, always think of this, of what you are doing now for us here. You have brought help and comfort where it is so sadly needed.'

And the need was great indeed. As his physical state

deteriorated, the patient's spirits sank even lower, and the adjustment that they were hoping for seemed no nearer.

His wife and Angus agreed that they should each of them have some time out of the house every day – 'for fresh air and exercise,' was how they put it, but both of them knew that even more important was the need for a break from the constant scolding and complaining.

Angus remembered how much they had all laughed, even during the darkest days of the war, and how he had appreciated their wit and humour. I wish I could make them laugh now, he thought. There's a terrible need for laughter in this house. He wondered whether he should try playing the clown a little. But he was not a clown by nature, and the situation in the house did nothing to help.

Instead he decided to play about with the language as much as possible. His speech became full of puns, of deliberate mistakes. He found it quite easy to make Mme Mercier laugh by these means, and she soon realized what was going on and joined in, hoping to rekindle her husband's former love of a joke. Nothing seemed to pierce his gloom, but at least the other two felt a little less weighed down by it.

Angus had never had to endure the trial of watching a slow death before. He had become well acquainted with death in its sudden, violent forms during his three wars, and also at the time of Nancy's suicide. But this was something quite new to him. He had often wondered at the equanimity of some of his comrades in the field as they faced imminent death – Bob, for instance, whose sole concern had been the thought of Dick's safety. It should be easier if you have plenty of warning, he had thought. Now he began to suspect that perhaps it's actually more difficult if you have warning. Because there's nothing of the big occasion about it, no supreme moment. The adrenalin doesn't keep on flowing for months at a time. After he came to this conclusion he found it less hard to keep his patience with the cantankerous old man.

On one occasion he was sitting up late at night with M. Mercier, who had been complaining continually. Angus suddenly felt that sleep was overpowering him. He sat up with a jerk, to shake himself awake. The old man noticed the movement and interpreted it correctly.

'So,' he exclaimed, 'you find it hard, do you? What do you think it's like for me? You want to sleep, and you can't. I want to sleep too. And no-one's going to come into the room in an hour or so and take my turn at dying. Dying', he went on, 'is a remarkably difficult business. I sometimes wonder whether I can actually go through with it.' He said this with a completely straight face. But Angus thought he caught a glimpse of the once habitual twinkle in the old man's eye, and burst out laughing. To his relief M. Mercier laughed too.

The following day Angus told Marie's mother about the little incident.

'*Dieu merci*,' she exclaimed. 'He has been so long without laughing, poor man. Perhaps he will adjust after all, as you say.'

From then on the sparks of humour continued, though only at intervals. There were long stretches of nothing but complaints and misery; but there was always the next flash of humour to look forward to, or the last one to chuckle over. As the illness progressed, and the pain became more intense, the patient was put on increasingly heavy sedation and began to spend a good part of every day sleeping.

On one occasion Angus was sitting with him in silence, and thought he must be asleep. But suddenly the old man opened his eyes and spoke in a perfectly normal voice:

'What will happen to me after I die?'

'We'll bury you.'

'Naturally. But the rest of me? The part you can't bury, what will happen to that?'

Angus shook his head. 'I don't know. Do you think anybody knows?'

'The priests say they know. According to them I'm bound to go straight to hell. After all, I've never paid any attention to them, and if they're right I'll be in a bad way, won't I?'

Angus side-stepped the issue. 'But do you believe what they say?'

'I never have. But now . . . I'd hate to find out they were right after all. It would be a bit late then, wouldn't it?'

'Well, there's always the option of a deathbed conversion.' Angus suggested this half in jest.

'That's always seemed a very cowardly thing to me. But then, I've never been about to die before. Eternity is a long, long time.' After a pause he said, 'What would you do if you were in my position – dying, an unbeliever, and yet not wanting to be consigned to everlasting hellfire?'

'I think I'd hope for the best.'

'Yes,' said the dying man, 'that certainly is an elegant solution. I think I shall adopt it. But if it turns out that the priests were right, if I am condemned . . . ' He smiled a mischievous smile and pointed an accusing finger at Angus.

'If you are condemned, then you must certainly lay the blame on me. It may not save you, but at least we shall have the pleasure of each other's company in hell.'

'And of a few other choice spirits too. Voltaire . . . and others . . . no doubt a few of the popes themselves. Oh, we shall be in distinguished company.' The sick man mused on in a contented manner for some time, gradually getting sleepy. At last the murmuring stopped and his eyes closed.

Angus was left wondering whether he had said the right thing. When he told Mme Mercier about the conversation, later on, she smiled. 'Yes, I'm sure that was the best thing to say. Yes, that's it, to hope for the best. If he had asked me, that's what I should like to think I'd have said. But I might not have thought of it. Or I might have lost my nerve and said I thought we should send for a priest, just in case. And that would be a denial of everything either of us has always believed.'

The bouts of ill temper continued, but they were interspersed with moments of more equable mood. During one of these the patient said to his wife:

'What will you do after I'm dead? You can't stay on in this big house alone.'

'No. Annette has asked me to go and live with them. After all, once the baby arrives, it will be quite useful having another woman in the house.'

'So!' he said, and they could hear from that one syllable that all the anger and bitterness was back in his voice. 'So you have made your plans. So you are just waiting for me to get out of the way and then you'll go off and start a new life without me in Toulouse. Without me,' he repeated savagely.

Mme Mercier and Angus exchanged a look of discouragement. Then Angus spoke:

'Why did you ask, if you don't want to know?'

'Ah yes,' said the old man. 'Why am I not behaving like a reasonable, considerate human being? I'll tell you why. Because what is happening to me is neither reasonable nor considerate.' His voice had gradually gained in volume, and he was now shouting at them. 'It is unreasonable and outrageous. It is cruel, unthinkably cruel. Am I so much worse than other people, that I should be made to suffer like this? All this pain, and the knowledge that it will get worse and worse, until I die. And what have I done to deserve this? Am I so much worse than you, my wife, who are busily making plans for a happy future? By what right, I ask you, by what right are you looking forward to more life, when I have to face death? You promised to share your life with me. Why are you not prepared to share my death? Why are your thoughts away from me already?' He had raised himself on one elbow, and was coughing and still trying to speak, but the words were unintelligible.

Between them Angus and Mme Mercier managed to get him to lie down again. His wife sat down on the bed beside him, took hold of one of his hands, and held it in hers. 'Rest, my dear, rest,' she said. Almost at once he closed his eyes and looked as if he had fallen asleep. But he opened them again and pressed her hand. Then he closed them and fell asleep.

After that he stopped eating, and spent more and more time sleeping.

When their old friend Dr Leroy came to see his patient he nodded gently and said:

'Yes, yes, the machine is running down. It won't be long now.'

The sick man opened his eyes and said:

'Good, good. That's want I wanted to hear.'

The machine hung on for another ten days, with sleep taking up most of the twenty-four hours. They never knew exactly when he died. But one cold morning in March his two nurses sat in the kitchen waiting for Dr Leroy to come and confirm the death. It was well under six months since the illness had been diagnosed.

After the funeral Angus wanted to travel with Mme Mercier on her journey to Toulouse, but she refused to consider such a thing.

'We have taken up enough of your time as it is. You must get back to your own life now.'

'What life?' asked Angus. 'I have no life of my own.'

'Yes, you have. You must get back to your roots. Roots are important.'

'You are having to leave yours. You have spent all your life in Rouen.'

'Yes, and because of that I have been able to grow firm and steady, like a strong healthy plant. I think I can survive being transplanted. And it won't be long till there is a new life to love. My first grandchild, just think!'

They both left Rouen on the same day, she to travel south, Angus bound for England. He couldn't help reflecting that, of the two of them, it was the woman, a generation older than he was, twice bereaved in the recent past, who was setting off with the more positive approach to her new life.

He knew now that he must go back to Kintalloch. Everything seemed to point him in that direction. But he was filled with doubts and misgivings. He had no idea what sort of reception to expect; from his parents, from Gavin and Meg, from Louis. At the very least they would be angry at his long silence, leaving them to think he was dead. The more he thought about it, the more unforgivable it seemed. He could find no justification for it beyond his own rancour. He realized that his homecoming would bring a lot of problems with it, for him and for the family. Would they be sufficiently pleased to know he was still alive to be able to forgive him the years of silence?

Soon he would find out. But first he had two missions to accomplish – Dick's family to visit, and Bob's parents to find.

19

His depression began to lift as soon as he got to the Essex village where Dick's parents lived. Suddenly he was in what looked like a Christmas-card world. It was a clear, frosty day with a blue sky, and the fields and trees were all white with hoar frost. The houses looked neat and well kept, the gardens trim and orderly. The scene formed a striking contrast to the tragic destruction he had seen in Rouen and the squalid state of post-war London. This was evidently a prosperous, well-heeled village that had lost no time in shaking off the aftereffects of the war.

He only had to ask once to find where Dick's house was. It turned out to be a large Georgian building set in its own grounds. Angus rang the bell and was greeted by a handsome middle-aged woman. He felt some trepidation about introducing himself. If Dick had indeed been killed he knew that his appearance would be bound to awaken painful memories. He thought that the best thing would be simply to tell them he had been a comrade-in-arms of Dick's, and just take it from there.

'My name's Angus Lindsay,' he said, 'and I was . . . '

But he got no further. The woman looked at him in astonishment and said:

'We thought you were dead. Dick told us you were killed in the action in which he was wounded. I just can't believe it. He'll be so pleased to see you! Oh, there he is. Dick! Dick! Come and see who's here!'

Angus turned and saw a tall figure approaching at a combination of a run and a slide, with an entourage of children laughing and shouting as they followed him by the same unsteady means of progress.

'They're my grandchildren,' explained the lady.

'Not . . . not Dick's?'

'No, my elder son's children. They adore Dick.'

It took a long time for each to get over his surprise and joy at finding that the other was still alive, and even longer to catch up on all the news they had to exchange.

Dick, it appeared, had been wounded during the first attack as the planes flew past, and was lying unconscious when Angus called him. After the second attack was over and the planes had gone, the survivors had got back into the truck, taking with them the wounded – or at least those they recognized as still alive.

'And Bob?' Dick asked. 'We thought you'd both been killed. Was he . . . ?'

'Bob really was killed. I can vouch for that. His last thoughts were for you. He was concerned about your safety. I promised I'd look after you. And then the second attack came, and that was that. So here I am, nearly eight years later . . . '

Dick explained that his wound had not been serious, and that he'd got back to England all in one piece.

'And then it all started up again with our war, you know. But I got home in time to start the term at Oxford last autumn. So I'm back at the grindstone now.'

'And still enjoying it?'

'More than ever.'

The family were so delighted to see Angus that they insisted he should spend the whole day with them, and even pressed him to stay for a few days. But Angus was anxious to get started on the quest for Bob's family.

'You don't happen to know their address, do you?' he asked Dick.

'No. All I know is that they live, or lived, in Bradford. Not a lot to go on, is it?'

Angus sighed. 'I think it may take me quite a while to find them.'

Sitting in the train on his way back to London that evening, Angus felt as if he'd spent the day in an enchanted world. All the children seemed to be rosy-cheeked and laughing, all the adults happy and serene. And Dick, who, in spite of his twenty-eight years, still seemed to be halfway between child and adult, had preserved all his boyish enthusiasm for poetry, for university life, for his parents, for the world in general.

In spite of the task that awaited him in Bradford, in spite of his own uncertain future, Angus was delighted, almost elated, by this glimpse into a harmonious world.

In Bradford he took a room in a modest bed-and-breakfast establishment. He knew his search might take him a long time, and he didn't want to arrive penniless at Kintalloch. He had just about exhausted the money in his name in the Paris bank, and he had nothing in this country.

On the day after his arrival he went to the main branch of the public library and told the young lady at the desk about his problem. She sent him to the reference department, where another young lady looked sympathetic but not hopeful.

'Telephone directory?' she suggested.

'Probably not. I don't think they're the kind of people that are likely to have a phone. Distinctly not middle-class.'

'Pity,' said the girl, then added hastily, 'I mean about the phone, of course.'

'Of course,' said Angus.

'Well, that leaves the voters' roll. Only it goes by streets, not names. Could take a long time to hunt up all the Grays.'

'A long time,' agreed Angus. 'Nothing else?'

'There's the valuation roll. But that also goes under streets.'

'Bother,' said Angus.

'Yes, a lot of bother,' agreed the girl.

'Perhaps the best thing', suggested Angus, 'would be to work with both the voter's roll and the telephone directory, and cut out all the Grays that are on the phone.'

The girl looked a bit doubtful. 'Well, it might save a lot of running around. But what if it turns out that they are on the phone after all?'

'I see what you mean.' Angus sighed.

'No idea where he worked? You might be able to trace his family through his employers.'

'That's an idea. He told me he worked in a textile factory.'

The girl rolled her eyes expressively. 'In Bradford? There are literally hundreds of mills in Bradford. That's why we exist, you might say. Goes back centuries. To the wool trade, to be exact.'

'Really! What a well informed young lady you are!'

'Thank you. Even if I don't seem able to provide the information you happen to need. Did he say anything about the factory? Its size, for instance?'

'I think he said it was a big one.'

'And did he say what his job was there?'

'Yes,' said Angus, relieved to be able to give a satisfactory answer at last. 'Accounts. He said he was in charge of the accounts.'

'Well, that narrows it down a bit. I suggest we work out a list of all the really big firms, and you go and make inquiries there. If you get nowhere you can come back and we'll work out a list of the not quite so big ones. How will that do?'

'Excellent. Looks as if I might be keeping you busy for some time, making out lists.'

The girl smiled and looked as if she didn't object to the prospect. Actually, he thought, I wouldn't at all mind if we had to have another session or two. She seems a remarkably nice girl.

Angus spent several days working his way through that first list. It was amazing how reluctant most of the firms were to give any information at all.

He had only two names left on the list, and was congratulating himself on the prospect of going back and getting a second list from the girl, when he struck gold. In the first place, he was able to contact the competent clerk without the usual difficulty, and in the second, the man looked up eagerly as soon as he heard Bob's name mentioned.

'Bob Gray? Yes, I remember him all right. Nice chap, Bob. A thoroughly decent fellow. Killed in the Spanish Civil War, wasn't he?'

They chatted a while about Bob, and then the clerk went and looked up the address. 'There you are,' he said as he handed Angus a slip of paper. 'Mind you, that was years ago. His people may have moved. I heard that the father had retired, so that may not be the right address any more. But if they've moved the new tenants might be able to tell you where they are now. If not . . . Needle in a haystack, eh? Hope you find them.'

Angus told himself that he ought to be feeling relieved and

elated, now that he actually had an address. It seemed that the hunt might well be over. But instead of relief and elation, he found he felt rather flat and apprehensive. Flat because he had lost his excuse for going to see the girl in the library again, and apprehensive about the meeting with Bob's parents.

His visits to the mills had given him a good idea of the lay-out of Bradford, and he had no difficulty finding the street. It consisted of opposite rows of very small red-brick terraced houses. They were obviously very old, and had not aged gracefully. A few more years, he thought, and this will all be slum property.

He rang the bell and waited. The door was opened by an elderly man with a cap on his head and slippers on his feet. The upper part of his body was clad in an ill-fitting, shapeless sort of cardigan.

'Yes?'

'Are you Mr Gray?' Angus hoped this wasn't Mr Gray.

'Yep. That's me. What is it?'

'My name's Angus Lindsay. I fought beside your son Bob in Spain.'

'Come in,' said the man severely, and stepped aside to let Angus into the tiny hall.

Mr Gray pushed open a door that led into what was obviously the living room, and called out:

'Gert. Someone to see you.'

Both Angus and Mr Gray were still standing at extremely close quarters in the little hall while they waited for the arrival of Bob's mother. In a moment she shuffled into the living room, wiping her hands on her apron. Her appearance was a little less slipshod than her husband's, but it was clear that she had spent little time or money on it. She looked harassed and slightly apprehensive, but her manner was less curt than that of her husband. When Angus had explained his mission she gave her husband a quick, almost frightened look, and then asked Angus to come in and sit down.

He found it extraordinarily difficult to speak about Bob to this extinguished-looking old couple. Neither had anything to say as they listened, no questions to ask. The mother was obviously less hostile than the father, but still not in the least forthcoming. Angus spoke as much as he could in the middle of this discouraging silence. He talked of Bob's good humour, his intelligence, his courage, the way the other men looked up to him, and of how his last words had expressed concern for a young comrade. He felt as if he were living in some sort of nightmare world, where he had to go on talking all the time, even when he could think of nothing more to say. At last he stopped.

And then Mr Gray began. He cleared his throat noisily, put down the folded newspaper that had been in his hand since he opened the door, and said:

'I suppose you think we ought to be grateful to you for coming and telling us all this. As if we didn't know what Bob was like. As if we'd forgotten. As if we could forget. One son we had, Mr . . . Mr . . . '

'Lindsay,' prompted Angus.

'Mr Lindsay. One son. And we lost him. Do you think we'd be living like this, in this hole of a place, if he'd still been alive, with his good wages? If Bob was still here we'd be living at the other end of Bradford, in one of them nice two-up, two-down houses, with a proper bathroom. Not this old slum. But that's it, he's dead now, and we're stuck here for the rest of our natural. Have a look, have a good look at this room. Spacious, isn't it?' His voice rang out in its irony. 'Well, that's just about all there is to the house. A lean-to kitchen at the back, and two bedrooms upstairs – two, mind you – two bedrooms and a landing all squeezed into the size of that there ceiling. Great, isn't it? I suppose you could say it was nice and snug, eh? Not a lot to heat, anyway. But would you call this snug, eh? Just that miserable little coal fire, and that's it. That's all the heating in the whole house. How would you like to live like that? No thank you, it wouldn't do for a fine gentlemen like you. But that's the way we live because that's all we can afford. And it won't get any better, will it? We're a bit too old to go out and look for jobs, Gert and me. Nobody would take us. So we sit here, and we watch one little bit of the house after another falling off, but we can't afford to do anything about it because repairs is too expensive, and landlords don't give a damn. Now, if Bob was with us . . .

'Great hopes we had in Bob. He was good to his parents, he was. And he'd have gone far. He was a bright lad, he was.'

Angus tried to murmur something in agreement, but Mr Gray ignored him. It seemed that Angus had had his turn, and now he was to be the listener. Mrs Gray sat through both halves of the conversation in complete silence, her face utterly expressionless. Poor woman, thought Angus, I wonder how often she has to listen to this.

'And it's not as if I hadn't done my share,' Mr Gray went on relentlessly. 'I did my bit in the Great War. Four years in the trenches, I did. And not a word of thanks did I get for it. And this is what my grateful country thinks I deserve. Just look at it. More smoke than heat in that there fire, and a draught like a howling gale at the back of my neck because the windows don't fit and no-one's going to do anything about them. It's good enough for the likes of us, that's what it is. And if Bob hadn't gone and got himself killed he'd have done something about it. Handy with his hands, was Bob.

'And then the likes of you comes with your fine accent and your gentlemanly airs and tries to tell me all about my son.

I know what he was like. I know what I've lost. I've lost everything I had. Everything. Even my self-respect.'

Suddenly the diatribe was over. Mr Gray folded his hands over his stomach and gazed fixedly at the fire. There was a prolonged silence. Angus was afraid to get up and take his leave in case the old man meant to start again. But he took his cue from Mrs Gray, who asked him in a thin, papery sort of voice, like a mouse rustling in a corner, if she could make him a cup of tea. He declined, saying he really must be going, and then stood up and said goodbye to Mr Gray, who acknowledged this attention with a grunt as he picked up his paper again.

Mrs Gray had moved to the door and opened it to let Angus out. She followed him into the hall and closed the living-room door behind her, murmuring something about keeping out the draught. Then she opened the front door and stepped outside into the street with Angus. Looking apprehensively towards the house, she said:

'He wasn't always like that. He was a nice man, very contented and hard-working. But it's Bob's death has turned him like this. Bitter, very bitter. I mean, the house isn't that bad, not for working people like us.'

Angus expressed his regret and was about to take his leave when the woman spoke again. 'You young men that go off to fight other people's wars,' she said, 'do you never think of what you're leaving behind you? Do you never think of your own people?'

For a moment Angus was nonplussed. Then, thinking of Bob and his ideals, he said:

'I think Bob really was trying to think of his own people. But he didn't think of them in terms of country, he thought in terms of class. It was his own class he went out to fight for. His own people.'

Mrs Gray looked up at him, and he saw that the hard, strained lines of her face had softened. 'Yes,' she agreed, 'his own people.' She smiled, and Angus suddenly saw Bob's smile in front of him again. 'Thank you,' she said. 'And now I must go in again. You've seen what he's like.'

20

Angus parted from the old lady with his feelings in a state of complete turmoil. His sorrow over Bob's death was renewed, fresh, as if his friend had only died that very day. His long monologue on the subject of Bob's virtues had brought the dead man back to him in vivid detail. And then that smile on his mother's face, Bob's own sudden, almost impish smile.

The stress of having to go on talking into the obdurate silence, trying to forget his own emotion, had left him weak and shaken. And there were so many other things that he should have said, had he known how the interview was to go, had he known that, having stopped speaking, he was not to be allowed to begin again.

In the midst of his distress over that unhappy meeting he was also aware of the almost farcical element of the conversation. There had been no exchange of views or sentiments, not till the last few words out in the street with Bob's mother. The rest had been nothing but two juxtaposed and practically unrelated soliloquies. Their order could have been reversed and it would have made no difference. They could even have run concurrently.

For years he had been thinking of the conversation in which Bob had asked him to go and see his parents. He remembered asking whether there was to be any message, and Bob saying, 'Just tell them . . . ' And he, Angus, had confidently promised. 'I'll tell them,' he had said, sure that the right words would come if the occasion should arise. Well, after all those years, it had arisen, and it had passed, and he had muffed it. He had not been able to say any of the things that he had felt sure Bob wanted to say. He had muffed it. But how could he have foreseen the bizarre rules by which the conversation was to be run? The old man's voluble hostility and the woman's intimidated silence?

And then, as he thought of the woman, and of the final words they had exchanged in the street, he was able to take some comfort from the fact that he had managed to say a little of what Bob might have wanted him to say. He had at least managed to say enough to raise that sudden shadow of Bob's smile on his mother's faded face.

But how sad it was, how futile and sad, that two people should be living like this, both victims of the old man's paranoia. He thought of Bob, of his wit and good humour, of his wide and hopeful horizons, and it seemed doubly tragic that the parents of such a man should have come to this. 'You young men that go off to fight other people's wars,' his mother had said. Suddenly it seemed to him that freedom, equality, communism, and all the other flag-flying ideals had a lot to answer for.

What, he wondered, would the situation have been like in this home if Bob had still been alive? There would have been a little more material prosperity, of that there could be no doubt. But what about the old man's state of mind? Would he have retained the contentment of previous years? Or was his state due to some form of mental decay? Would he just have found something else to feel aggrieved about? But even if that were the case, poor Mrs Gray would at least have had

Bob's company to help her bear her husband's infirmity. And she would have had enough money to light a decent fire.

He had been shocked by the meanness and dinginess and lack of any kind of ease and comfort in that home. He remembered his conversation with Bob about the haves and have-nots, and it seemed to him that Bob had lied when he said that his home was borderline. Even assuming that more money must have been coming into the house when Bob was living at home, by no stretch of the imagination could that poky little house – in that shabby, depressed little street – belong to any but the have-nots. But then it all depended on where you stood when you made the assessment. He had never thought of his family as well off, and yet to Bob they seemed to possess untold wealth. And he sighed, as he thought of how little people know of each other.

Once again he remembered the trance-like happiness of his visit to Dick and his family. The comfort and abundance that surrounded them had seemed to him at the time perfectly normal and ordinary. Now it seemed to him that those people lived in a state of blind, self-indulgent luxury, in their own comfortable, pampered world, unaware of the hardship and poverty round about them. Because they must, surely, be unaware of it. Otherwise, how could they go on living such disproportionately affluent lives? They were decent people, lovely people, full of charm and kindness and friendliness. They couldn't possibly know that their gracious and abundant way of life rested on a basis of such meanness and deprivation. And yet, and yet . . . They were intelligent people too, well read, well informed.

And then Angus thought of his own family, and the contrast with what he had just seen was equally striking and equally mortifying.

In spite of the cold of the evening air, he sat down on a bench to try to straighten out the agitated tangle of thoughts inside him. He closed his eyes and tried to follow where his thoughts were leading him. Am I preaching communism to myself, he wondered. And then he remembered that only a few minutes ago he had dismissed communism and all the other isms as responsible for the tragedy of war. More confused and angry than ever, he stood up and began walking again.

In the end he came to the conclusion that he was overwrought, and had better forget about the matter for the time being. The prospect of this meeting had been weighing on his mind for many years. It was not surprising that he should be experiencing some sort of reaction now. Especially given the distressing nature of the interview.

Besides, he reminded himself, now that this is over, you really are at a crossroads. You've accomplished all the tasks you meant to do before you could go back to Kintalloch. You've tied up all the loose ends. There's nothing to keep you back now. Are you really going?

For a long time everything and everyone seemed to have been pointing him in this direction – the shepherd, Mme Mercier, Annette and Pierre, with the thought of their unborn child adding to his awareness of the importance of the family, of the continuity of the race . . . It had all culminated in the happy family atmosphere of his visit to Dick. When he had set off for Bradford there was no doubt in his mind that the next step would be Kintalloch. And now Bradford and what he had found there had filled his mind with an endless array of doubts – doubts that rested not on his own individual preferences, but on moral issues that had nothing to do with either his own hopes or his own weaknesses.

He walked the streets of Bradford that night till he was too exhausted to think any more. When at last he got back to his bed-and-breakfast he went straight to bed, too tired even to face the landlady and her late-evening cup of tea.

By the following morning Angus had dealt with the problems of his irreconcilable beliefs in the way he had dealt with such problems since his youth – he had decided to take a fatalistic view of the matter and let things straighten themselves out as best they could. He was going to take things as they came.

And the first thing he meant to take was a little pleasant conversation with the girl in the library. After all, it would only be polite to go and tell her that her efforts had been successful. The least he could do was go and thank her. In reality he had it in his mind to do a little more than that. He might ask her out for a meal. And that, assuredly, would be the end of it. One pleasant meal out, and end of chapter. He was in no position to get involved with another woman. Besides, there was Marie. This was only going to be a one-off occasion, a pleasant interlude after a very trying time and before . . . before what?

He made straight for the reference department of the library, and was a little put out to find another young lady there. When she offered her assistance he explained that he particularly wanted to see the same young lady he had seen a few days before, about some information she had given him.

'Which one would that be? Do you know her name?'

'No, I'm afraid not.'

'Well, there are only two others. Was she small and fair or tall and dark?'

'Small and fair.'

'That would be Mrs Daniels. I'm afraid she's not on duty today. Would you like to leave a message?'

In view of the information he had just been given Angus

decided that the only sensible message to leave was simply to please tell Mrs Daniels that her list had had the right name in it, and that there would be no need for a further list. And to thank her very much.

He left the building feeling disappointed and at the same time angry with himself – for being disappointed, and for not having noticed that the girl was wearing a wedding ring. You're no better than a teenager, he told himself severely. And then he seemed to catch a glimpse of Marie's face, smiling ironically. It would only have been the one evening, he assured her. After all, I'm leaving tomorrow. Going back to Kintalloch.

Sans blague? said Marie. And her expression became even more ironical.

He went straight to the station to find out about the first possible train for Edinburgh.

You see? he said to Marie. *Sans blague.*

21

Gavin had just made his early morning cup of tea. Ever since his marriage it had been tacitly agreed that he would see to himself first thing in the morning. Even his mother, that indefatigable matron, had accepted that it was better to let him have the run of the kitchen till he went out for his before-breakfast round of the estate, as his father and his grandfather had done before him. 'I don't think he likes having anyone else around till he's awake,' Bessie had joked, and Meg had agreed with her mother-in-law.

'Not exactly chatty, first thing in the morning,' had been her comment.

He had just taken his first sip when he heard the phone ring. A bit early for phone calls, he thought, as he picked up the receiver.

'Gavin Lindsay here.'

There was a slight pause, and then a voice said:

'Gavin, this is Angus.'

'Angus!' Gavin nearly shouted the word in his astonishment.

'Yes, I know, you must have thought I was dead. I suppose. And I very nearly was.'

'And where the hell have you been ever since?'

'Everywhere, nowhere . . . I'll explain later. Can I come to Kintalloch?'

'Of course you can come to Kintalloch. You *must* come to Kintalloch.'

'Well, that's a relief.'

'Don't be an idiot. When can you get here? Where are you?'

'Edinburgh.'

'Can you catch the seven-fifty train?'

'I think I can just about make it.'

'Right. I'll meet you at the station here. By the way, you won't have had any news, I suppose, wherever you've been.'

'No. Any changes?'

'Mum died.'

'Mum! Mum, not Dad?'

'No. He's still with us, but frail. Mum died some five years ago. I thought I'd better warn you.'

As he made his way up the stairs Gavin was wondering how he should break the news to the rest of the family. Three generations, he thought. Where do I start?

In the bedroom he found Meg awake, thinking about getting up.

'Who was that, phoning so early?'

Gavin hesitated. 'A voice from the past. Almost a voice from the grave, you could say.'

Meg heard the emotion in his voice and sat up suddenly in bed.

'You don't mean . . . Angus?'

'Yes. He's in Edinburgh. I'm to pick him up at the station later this morning.'

'Is he all right?'

'Seems to be.'

'But where has he been all these years?'

'He hasn't explained yet. I expect he'll be hearing the question rather often once he gets here. I told him about Mum.'

'That's going to be a problem, isn't it? Do we tell him what we think?'

'That she died of a broken heart, because of him? A bit cruel, don't you think?'

Meg nodded. 'Yes. We can't ask anybody to live with that. And anyway, it's only what we think. The death certificate said influenza.'

'Do you think the others will tell him – about the broken heart, I mean? My father, for instance.'

'I just don't know. He took her death so well. But perhaps this idea is still rankling. We'll be all right with Louis, anyway.'

'Oh yes,' said Gavin. 'He adores his father. *He* won't spill the beans.'

Meg had got out of bed by this time and was standing at the window looking out thoughtfully. 'I wonder. He worships the hero who was killed in battle. What will he make of the real man?'

'What are *we* to make of him, if it comes to that?' Gavin suddenly laughed. 'Trust Angus,' he said, and laughed again.

Meg ran over to where her husband was standing and put her arms round him. 'Oh, Gavin, I'm so glad for you. And for us all, once we get over the initial shock, that is. Do you think he'll stay this time?'

'Who can tell? Not even Angus, I suppose.'

Tom heard the news of his son's return from the presumed grave with surprising composure.

'The thing is,' he said in explanation, 'once you're as old as I am, you don't really believe all that much in death. Take Bessie, now. I know she died five years ago. I know it in here,' and he tapped his forehead. 'But it's a different story in here,' he said, as he laid a hand on his heart. 'And it's been rather the same with Angus. You believe it, yes, but . . . but it's not the only truth. And anyway,' he added, coming back to everyday reality, 'where's the young scamp been all this time?'

'The young scamp in question,' said Gavin, 'is now forty-seven years old, and no doubt able to tell you himself. So far we have no idea.'

Just then Louis appeared.

'Has *he* been told yet?' asked Tom.

When Louis came in Meg had been just about to suggest that she should tell him in private. She really didn't know how the news would affect him. In spite of the boy's obvious admiration for the father-hero, she had not forgotten his early antagonism. But now it was too late for any gentle preparation.

'Been told what?' asked Louis.

There was a silence.

Meg broke it. 'We've just had a piece of joyful and very surprising news,' she said.

'Well, what is it?'

'I had a phone call this morning,' said Gavin. 'From your father.'

Louis's first reaction seemed to be disbelief. Then he suddenly turned crimson and walked over to one of the windows. He stood there looking out on to the lawn and muttered:

'I simply can't believe it.'

Meg walked over to him and put a hand on his arm. 'It's a big, big shock, isn't it? It will take us all a little time to adjust. But it's the most wonderful news, almost like a fairy tale.'

Louis turned round and faced the others. He was looking

more composed, though still flushed. 'He's coming here, is he?'

'Yes. I'm going to meet the train later on this morning,' said Gavin.

'I'll come too,' said Louis.

'Yes, yes, off you go, the lot of you. I'll see to the work,' joked Tom, who had taken no active part in the running of the estate for many a year.

'A well-run establishment like this can get by without supervision for an hour or two,' claimed Gavin. 'That right, Louis?'

'Do you think I should come too?' asked Meg.

'Why not? Let's make it a family party. Except for Dad, that is. We'll explain that he never leaves the house these days.'

Tom drew himself up to his full, frail height. 'He's leaving it today,' he said. 'I want everyone to know that I was glad to welcome my son home. If they see me there at the station, the whole village will soon know.'

22

On his way to Edinburgh Angus had spent a lot of time wondering how he should make the great disclosure to his family. There didn't seem to be any accepted formula for such a situation. He felt he ought to prepare them in some way for the discovery that he was not only still alive, but coming to see them. Only, he could think of no way of doing this. After all, he thought, you're either dead or not dead. There's no convenient halfway house that you can use to prepare the ground. He would just have to take the plunge.

Before his conversation with Gavin he had felt very apprehensive about his reception in Kintalloch. But Gavin's low-key reaction had reassured him somewhat. He was counting on the drive from the station to sound Gavin about how the others felt. Louis most of all, naturally.

The news of his mother's death had been a big shock to Angus. He had always thought of her as indestructible. Now he began to wonder whether his disappearance might have been a contributory factor. If so, there was not only his own sense of guilt to face up to, but also the fear that the others, especially his father, might hold this against him. He remembered how angry his father had been when he had left Kintalloch after his abortive attempt to settle down there and take his share in the running of the place. If only he'd been able to explain why he was leaving.

It was all his fault, of course. He should never have allowed the situation with Meg to develop as it did. But, since that had happened, the only thing he could do was go away. He had behaved badly, but not as badly as his father had thought. He had not given up his place in the family out of sheer frivolity. It was now more than twenty years since the episode with Meg, and Angus had gone over it in his mind again and again. He wondered whether Meg and he would ever be able to speak about it. During his brief visits to the family after Louis had come to live in Kintalloch the subject had never been mentioned between them.

Another taboo subject had been Louis's hostility to Angus. They had only discussed this at the very beginning, and had agreed that its cause probably lay in a confused recollection of the dramatic moments that had preceded Nancy's death. They had also agreed that it was better not to distress the child by telling him the truth about the mother he had loved so much and grieved over so bitterly. Perhaps, they had thought, perhaps when he was much older, better able to understand, they might tell him of her drink problem and her attempt at killing him just before taking her own life.

Angus was almost certain that Louis had never mentioned to the rest of the family that he had virtually told his father to stay away. Once again, he supposed, they had attributed an action on his part to the wrong cause. Not knowing his real reason for staying away, they had no doubt blamed his supposedly irresponsible attitude for his departure for Spain. Altogether, he felt they had much to forgive him, even without the sins which he had not in fact committed. He was immensely relieved that Gavin, at least, seemed to bear no rancour, and hoped the others felt the same. Except for Louis, of course. He could think of no reason why his son should have got over his antipathy.

Louis was having a difficult morning. The shock of discovering that his father was still alive brought with it a reassessment of the whole situation. After that last meeting with his father, when Angus had written to say he was joining the International Brigade, the child had felt almost certain that it was because his son had rejected him. He had felt a mixture of guilt and pride – pride in himself, when he thought of his power over this adult, and pride in his father for going off to the wars. When the news came that Angus was missing, presumed dead, Louis had only been able to cope with the sense of guilt this brought him by, as it were, canonizing his father. Gradually he came to see Angus as a combination of saint and hero, a shining Parsifal figure. Now the reality was rushing towards him and Kintalloch at sixty miles an hour, and Louis simply didn't know what to expect. In addition, he didn't know what to make of the fact that his father had stayed away all those years without even letting them know he was alive. Was this also because of him?

He worried all the way to the station and then, just as the train was due in, he made the sort of decision that was characteristic of his father when faced with an insoluble problem. He decided he would let it ride. He would just let things take their course and stop worrying about them.

There was a great flurry in Kintalloch station that morning, when the Lindsay family got out of the car and stood waiting on the platform. The Lindsays seldom left their own domain, and never en masse – it was the first time old Mr Lindsay had been seen for years.

What on earth could be going on?

Some of the more adventurous, or more curious, approached the family and tried to start up a conversation. They were answered with totally uncommunicative politeness, and had to withdraw uninformed. But all eyes were on the family when the train came in, and within minutes the whole village knew that Angus Lindsay, the second son, the black sheep, the hero, the adventurer, the prodigal, the square peg and good-for-nothing had come back. And if no-one had actually seen the fatted calf, there could be no doubt from the way his family had greeted him that it was certainly on the menu.

It took a long time for all the explanations and questions and exclamations to be dealt with. Most of the talking had to come from Angus, for little had happened in Kintalloch apart from Bessie's death and Louis's couple of years in the army. Angus gave them a potted account of his adventures and misadventures, but all the details were rationed out parsimoniously.

He had so much to explain that they decided that the best way would be to devote their evenings to listening to a minute account of all that had happened, starting from the beginning.

He told them about the Civil War, his rescue by Gil, his long convalescence, and his trek across the Pyrenees to Alphonse's hut. It was when he got to the next bit that he realized he was on more dangerous ground. During all these adventures he had really had no opportunity of contacting his people. But once he reached Paris, or even from Toulouse, he could have written to let them know he was still alive.

He waited for the unasked question, and it didn't come. He embarked on the story of his life in Paris with Marie, his work in the government office, then his concealment in Rouen under the Pétain government. Still no-one asked the awkward question.

At this point he broke off.

'Look,' he said, 'this is bloody silly. Does nobody really want to know why I didn't contact any of you before that?'

Tom looked at him sternly. 'Watch your language, young man. Ladies present.'

'I'm sorry. Anyway, I feel we must have an answer to the question nobody has been unkind enough to ask. I think perhaps it can come from Louis.'

Louis was staring fixedly at the fire. He had known that this moment was bound to come sooner or later. Now it was his turn to speak:

'You probably thought I didn't want you to come back because of what I said the last time you were here. And it's true, I didn't – then. But as time went on, and I knew you'd gone to fight in Spain, I began to change my mind. And when I heard you'd been killed, I felt terrible. But there was nothing I could do about it by then.'

'Thank you, Louis. And that's why I stayed away. It seemed to me that, since you all presumably thought I was dead anyway, the best thing was to remain dead for all family purposes. I was so sure that one person here didn't want me back.'

'And what made you change your mind?' asked Meg.

'Oh, things . . . things, all the things that have happened to me since then. We'll come to them all in time.'

'Before you go on to the next bit, Angus,' said his brother, 'I think there's a point we ought to try and clear up.'

Louis looked up. 'You mean, why did I not want Dad to come back?'

'Yes. Can you tell us why?'

'I'm honestly not sure I know. There's always been such a mystery about my mother's death. I have only the most confused impressions of that time, but I definitely had the feeling that she died because of an attack by my father. I see now – now that I'm beginning to know him – that this simply couldn't be the case. But that was what I thought. And you know how I loved my mother.'

It was Meg who spoke now:

'We never really knew what to do about that situation. I think we must have made the wrong decision. But you were so fond of your mother, and so grieved by her death . . . '

'We didn't want to disillusion you,' said Tom. 'I remember what an unhappy, frightened little waif you were when Gavin and his mother brought you back.'

'Well, who's going to tell me? Who's going to tell me the real story about my mother's death? She did fall from a balcony, didn't she? I'm sure I remember being on the balcony with her – and Dad.'

'I'll tell him,' said Gavin. 'I was there just after the event. I heard not only what your father said, Louis, but also what the neighbours and the police had to say. Your mother, I am sorry to tell you, was an alcoholic. On the day of her death she had been drinking heavily, and she had given you so much gin that you were in a drunken stupor. When your father got home and found out he threatened to send you here right away, to get you out of her control. Now, your mother was an unhappy woman, and she had this terrible affliction. But she was very fond of you. And the fear of losing you drove her to lock herself up in the bedroom with you. She then told your father he could speak to her from the balcony of the next room, while she stood holding you in her arms on the bedroom balcony. She told your father that she was going to throw you across to him. If he caught you, which would have been virtually impossible, you were to be his, and she would throw herself to the street. Well, she tried to throw you across, but the movement must have woken you up, and you caught hold of her hair. While she was struggling with you, trying to disentangle your hands, your father jumped over from the other balcony and seized you. He saved you, but he didn't manage to stop your mother from throwing herself over the balcony.'

There was a long silence.

Eventually Meg spoke:

'And that's the story we didn't dare tell you, because we knew how much you loved your mother.'

The evening that Angus had told them about Marie's death Meg and Gavin were on their way upstairs to bed, when she stopped on the landing, and said:

'I think I'll go back down and speak to Angus. He must miss her dreadfully. He was fond of Nancy, in a tormented, exasperated sort of way, but I don't think he's ever loved a woman as he loved Marie.'

'No, probably not. Poor Angus. Things never seem to work out for him, do they?'

Meg found Angus sitting alone in the library, looking at the fire. He seemed thoughtful and dispirited. He hadn't heard her come in, and looked up quickly when she approached.

'I thought you'd gone off to bed.'

'I'm just going. But I wanted to say how much I feel for you over Marie's death. She seems to have been a wonderful person.'

For answer, Angus took out his wallet and handed it to her, open. Inside was Marie's photograph. Meg sat for a long time looking at the beautiful, intense face.

'She's lovely,' she said, as she handed back the photograph, 'so full of life. It must be very hard for you.'

'You can imagine why I broke out after that and set off to join up with the *maquisards* to kill as many Germans as I could.' Angus was still staring at the photograph. 'You know how Dad says at times that he doesn't entirely believe that Mum is dead? Well, in a way I know what he means. There are times when I remember Marie so well that it's as if I were seeing her right in front of me, commenting on what's happening to me. There are even times when she seems to be having a little joke at my expense. A situation not unknown in the past,' he added with a smile.

'I'm glad you feel you have some sort of communication. I don't think I have this capacity. The only people I've really loved that have died, my parents and your mother, they all seem quite lost to me. Perhaps it's because I've never lost anyone who was as close to me as that, not in that way.'

'I can only hope you never will. You had enough sorrow when you lost your three unborn children.'

Meg stood up to go. 'There's something I've been meaning to say for a long time – years, actually.' She stopped speaking and stood staring at the fire for a moment.

'Yes?'

'I wanted to thank you for going away when you did. I thought it was terribly cruel of you at the time. But in the end I saw that it was the only thing to do. The only decent thing to do. And I want you to know that I've been grateful to you for a long time. I simply can't bear to think what sort of a mess I'd have made of my life if you'd let me run off with you.'

Angus gave a little sigh. 'I wonder whether Louis will ever be grateful to me for going off a second time.'

'I think he was grateful. Then, at least. He just couldn't cope with an intermittent father at the time.'

'Especially one he thought had murdered his mother. Poor Louis, it must have been hard for him.'

'Well, it's come all right in the end. He knows the true story, and he thinks you're wonderful.'

'Rather a dangerous belief, don't you think?'

'Well, that's up to you. All you have to do is go on being wonderful.'

'What could be easier?'

After the first few weeks of strangeness, things settled down and they all got used to the new routine. Tom said little, but it was clear that he took a good deal of satisfaction in having his errant son back in the fold. The others often noticed him looking at Angus, with a faint smile on his lips. Then he would nod gently, before going on with whatever he was doing.

Angus had a great deal to learn about the running of the estate. It was more than twenty years since he had taken any part in it, and things had changed enormously during that time. But a challenge was what Angus loved most on this earth.

'I'll soon be able to retire,' joked Gavin. 'With Angus here and Louis back from the army, who needs me?'

'Tell you what,' said Angus, 'why don't you take Meg off for a holiday somewhere?'

'That's an idea.' Gavin seemed quite taken with the thought. 'How about a week or two in gay Paree, Meg?'

'I'd love that. I've never been to France, and yet I've always wanted to go, ever since I was a schoolgirl. Miss Hamilton used to speak so much about it. I was lucky to have such a governess. She really taught me to love the language and the literature.'

'She certainly taught you to speak very good French,' agreed Angus. 'I really think you ought to go over and try it out.'

After some discussion it was agreed that the couple were

to go over to Paris for a few weeks in the autumn. Meanwhile Angus and Louis worked hard at learning all there was to know for the smooth running of the estate, and Meg hunted out her school books and started brushing up her French.

23

When the time came the couple went off, and the three remaining men found things a little dull without them.

'Well, you see,' said Tom one day when they were commenting on this, 'Meg's the old-fashioned sort of woman who really knows how to make a home. And the home just isn't right without her, is it?'

'Do you think he's pining for her?' Angus asked Louis one day, when Tom had seemed particularly quiet.

'Wouldn't be surprised. I'm sure he misses her more than he misses Uncle Gavin.'

'Yes, I'm sure he does. After all, he spends all day in the house, while we're out and about. And anyway, Meg's special. Who wouldn't miss her?'

Louis looked at his father speculatively. 'You know, I've sometimes wondered why you let Uncle Gavin marry her. Why you didn't marry her yourself.'

Angus burst out laughing. 'Let! Let him marry her! I had no choice in the matter. That's the problem with being the second son. A thing you know nothing about.'

Louis was looking at his father with evident hostility. 'Are you suggesting she married him for his position?'

'Good heavens, no. Never in a thousand years. She married

him because she was in love with him. No doubt whatever about that. And she fell in love with him – in the first place, at any rate – because he turned up and proposed to her on his way to the trenches in 1916, when she was only sixteen years old. Now, if I'd been able to go and propose to her in my officer's uniform, instead of the school uniform I was still wearing at the time, who knows, she might have accepted me.'

'But did you want to marry her?'

'The idea hadn't occurred to me. We were cousins and I was fond of her. But a year later I might have thought of it.'

'Probably just as well that didn't happen,' said his son charitably. 'You'd have led her a hell of a dance if she'd married you.'

'No doubt.'

Louis was not prepared to drop the conversation. 'Did you mind being the second son?' he asked.

'In some ways I minded a lot. That's probably why I stayed on in France after the war.'

'And do you mind now?'

'No, I can't honestly say that I do. As things have turned out, there really isn't much difference between us now, is there? I have my share in the family home, and the work, and the profits. About the only thing that would normally be different is that, if Gavin and Meg had any children, *their* eldest son would inherit.'

'But they haven't, and you have, so it's your son who inherits. Funny, isn't it?'

'So, you see, I can hardly be considered the second son any longer. More like first equal.'

'As if you were twins.'

'Well, we wouldn't have been the first twins in the family.

You know your grandfather and your great aunt Ellen were twins?'

'Yes, I've heard something about that.'

Angus noticed a touch of unexpected emphasis on the last word.

'What have you heard?'

'Just some unpleasant rumours. But I never managed to find out what they were about. Do you know?'

'Yes. The twins were wildly attached to each other, and the rumour got about that it was some sort of incestuous relationship.'

'Do you believe that?'

'No, certainly not. You know your grandfather so you can judge for yourself. As for Aunt Ellen, whom you never knew, I think I can vouch for her. So the best thing you can do is forget all about it. And, above all, don't speak a word about it to Meg. She doesn't know.'

'I wouldn't dream of it!' Louis's voice held all the indignation of the mature man who believes that women should be protected from such things.

What neither of them knew was that one of the chief sorrows of Meg's life had been the discovery, after her mother's death, of some poems which made it abundantly clear that Ellen's feelings for her brother were of an intensely passionate and carnal nature. She had burnt the papers and told no-one except Doc, Bessie's father, who for over fifty years had been the family doctor and confessor. She had never been able to mention the poems and the secret they revealed to anyone else, not even Gavin. The irony of it was that all the other members of the family knew about the rumours and conspired to keep the knowledge from Meg.

One evening after Tom had gone to bed, Angus and Louis

sat chatting by the fire till quite late. With Gavin and Meg away, father and son spent more time in each other's company, and the conversation about being a second son and about the past skeleton in the family cupboard had served to convince Louis that he could talk freely to his father and expect to be treated as an adult. Louis was kneeling by the fire, stirring up the dying embers, when he said in a tone of deep feeling:

'You're lucky, Dad. You've had three wars.'

'Not the sort of good fortune everybody appreciates,' Angus remarked, laughing. 'And after all, you've already had one. That's not bad, for your age.'

'I didn't have a proper one. Or rather, I didn't have a proper share of it. I only got the tail end. I wasn't even sent abroad. That's not what I call a war at all.'

'Well, that's one aspect in which I seem to have had all the luck, isn't it? I hope I'm duly grateful.'

'Oh, come on, Dad. Stop fooling. I'm sure you know what I mean.'

Angus sighed. 'Yes, Louis, I know what you mean. You mean that your life here is pleasant but dull. That you don't see any prospect of covering yourself with glory, or getting involved in any high adventure. Is that it?'

His son gave a sheepish smile. 'Well, yes, that's about it. And by the time there's another war I'll probably be too old for it – unless something unexpected turns up.'

'You mean another windfall like the Spanish Civil War, to top us up between our own wars?'

'Dad, I wish you'd stop joking about it. It's a serious matter.'

'I'm the last person to deny that war is a serious matter. I've seen far too much of it for that. But I see what you mean. It's serious for you because you feel that your life

181

here is too staid and comfortable and secure, and you don't see what you can do about it short of going off and fighting another war.'

'Well, what else is there to do? That's exciting and challenging, I mean.'

'I'm sure there must be something. Something less stupid and brutal and pointless than another war.'

'Dad! What a way to talk!. From you of all people! Do you mean to say you just didn't believe in the wars you were fighting?'

'At first, yes, I did. In the first war I had the conviction that we were fighting for the right, that to go off to the trenches to kill as many Germans as possible was a noble and worthy thing to do.

'War number two, the Spanish Civil War. You know why I went to fight in that one. Purely personal reasons. All I knew about the situation in Spain was just enough to make me feel I'd rather fight for the Republicans than for Franco, that was all. If I'd known how things were going to turn out, that all that carnage would be in vain, I hope I'd have had the guts to get out of it at once.

'As for the last war, again my motives for being involved in it were more personal than patriotic. I've told you about Marie. She was the sort of person that casts a spell over you, whose enthusiasm you just can't resist. She was passionately committed to defeating the Germans and so, as a result, was I. Marie would have had the most convinced pacifist throwing bombs. And that's why I joined in. But it was a purely emotional decision, not an ethical one.'

Louis was looking at his father in deep distress:

'Are you saying that, if we found ourselves in the middle of another war, you wouldn't join in?'

'I don't know. I really don't know whether I'd join in. The

one thing I'm sure of is that, on ethical grounds, I certainly *shouldn't* join in.'

'Nobody should, you mean?'

'Yes, I suppose that's what I mean.'

'You're a pacifist, then?'

'If you must put a label on me . . . '

'I must say, it's the last thing one would expect from a man with your history.'

'You saw nothing of the last war. You've just been complaining of precisely that yourself. If you had seen a bit more you would understand that it's precisely my history that made me feel as I do. If I hadn't taken part in the carnage and seen the dead and the dying and the devastation that war leaves, I'd no doubt still be happy to intone all the jingoistic slogans, I'd still be reading Rupert Brooke instead of Siegfried Sassoon and Wilfred Owen.'

Louis sighed.

Angus could see that he was deeply disappointed.

24

A few days later Meg and Gavin came back, delighted with their holiday. It didn't take Meg long to realize that there was something wrong with Louis, and she asked Angus about it.

'I'm afraid the honeymoon's over,' he said. 'I've fallen off my pedestal.'

'Oh, Angus, whatever have you done?'

'I've merely told him what I think of war.'

'And that is . . . ?'

'That it's indefensible.'

Meg was unable to repress a smile of amusement. 'I must say, coming from you . . . '

'I know. With my history . . . ? Exactly what Louis said. He's profoundly disappointed in me. He's made me feel like a terrible impostor, pretending to be a hero, when I'm nothing but an unspeakable coward.' He sighed. 'That's the worst of telling the truth.'

'It can't be that bad. He'll get over it. He's bound to accept you as you are — whatever that may be,' she added with a mischievous smile.

'You mean I'm a bit of a chameleon?'

'Well, you are, aren't you? And do you think you've convinced him about the futility of war?'

'I don't know. I don't even know whether to hope I have. The poor lad needs a war. He's longing for adventure, dying to prove himself, and what are the prospects?'

'He's really very like you. The difference is that you've never been short of wars. There's always been one handy when you needed it.'

'Lucky me!'

As time went on, it became clear that Louis was feeling more and more unsettled. They were all wondering what they could do about it, when their attention was diverted to a more urgent matter.

In spite of his frail health Tom always came down for breakfast with the rest of the family. One day he appeared looking very flushed and more unsteady than usual. Louis was just in time to grab his arm and prevent him from falling as he crossed over to his place at the table. He was immediately sent to bed and the doctor was summoned. By that time it was clear that he was in a very feverish state, sometimes sleeping, sometimes half awake. The doctor's examination roused him enough for him to ask:

'Well, young man, what is it?'

'Just a touch of flu. You'll have to stay in bed for a few days.'

'Flu!' exclaimed the patient. 'The same as Bessie.' And he smiled.

The family took it in turn to sit up with him all night. In the early hours of the morning, while Meg sat with him, he opened his eyes, looked at her, and said something Meg wasn't able to make out. She did catch the name Bessie, and wondered whether his mind was wandering and he had taken her for his wife. For a few minutes he kept up what sounded like a gentle conversation, so whispered that Meg was unable to make out more than the odd word. Then he fell asleep and never woke up again.

After the funeral, as they sat talking about him, Gavin said:

'You know, if there's such a thing as a saint, I think Dad was just about one of them. He was so gentle, so reasonable, even in his anger, so good-humoured and full of fun – indeed, so happy.'

'Yes,' said Angus, 'I'm sure that's one of the marks of the saint. Happiness.'

'It's funny,' said Meg. 'He and my mother were so fond of each other, and yet so different in spite of being twins. I don't think my poor mother could count as a saint on the happiness score, at any rate. Looking back, I can't think of any time I got the impression that she was happy.' She thought of the tormented poetry her mother had left behind her, and shook her head sadly. All four of them, remembering what being twins had meant to the brother and sister, thought of the incest rumours, and wondered why all the happiness seemed to have fallen to Tom.

A few weeks later, when Louis had gone out for the evening, the other three sat together, trying to find some solution to the problem of the young man's evident boredom and dissatisfaction.

'He won't think of going to university, anyway,' said Gavin. 'I think we've all tried to persuade him. Not adventurous enough, he says.'

'And he won't go off on a long holiday, just to see the world. Too pointless, he says,' added Angus. 'And I see what he means.'

'Yes,' agreed Meg. 'He's not frivolous enough for that. He needs a sense of purpose. Any other suggestions?'

'Well, he's not dedicated enough for Good Works,' said

Angus, 'so all sorts of voluntary organizations are out. Can you see him leading the local Boy Scouts?'

'Wish I could,' said Gavin. 'It would at least give him something to do with his spare time.'

'Yes, but not with his burning ambition,' pointed out Angus. After a while he spoke again. 'I've toyed with one idea. But perhaps it's too harebrained.'

'Sounds hopeful,' said Gavin. 'Let's hear it.'

'Well, remember Gil and Marta, the two Catalan peasants who took me in and nursed me back to life? It was a great sorrow to me when I left them, to think that I'd never see them again. And it was almost as bad to know that, even if I did manage to get out of the country alive, I'd never be able to contact them in any way, to let them know I'd made it. Remember they told me that even sending a letter would compromise them. They had risked so much by hiding me there. Now, things being as they are in Spain, there's not the slightest chance they'd ever let me into the country again, with my International Brigade history. But . . . ' Here he paused, and Gavin broke in:

'You think Louis might go?'

'Why not? It would be quite an adventure.'

'But, Angus, would it be safe?' Meg was evidently worried already at the prospect.

'It would be all right for him. He's got no criminal antecedents. They wouldn't even know I was his father. I gave my Paris address when I joined up. There's nothing to connect me with Kintalloch. Nothing to connect him with me.'

'Well . . . '

Gavin broke in again, laughing:

'If you want him to go, make sure you don't minimize the danger too much. That would make the scheme lose all its attractions.'

187

'Besides,' added Meg, more in favour of the plan now that it was presented as less hazardous, 'apart from the assumed danger, it has the advantage of having a purpose. Quite a romantic enterprise, in fact. And it links up with your own heroic exploits. He does want to be committed to something, poor darling.'

'I'd have liked to think he was committed to Kintalloch,' said Gavin.

'He is. He's devoted to Kintalloch,' said Angus. 'I'm sure you'll find that he is, in the long run. But Kintalloch doesn't really need him just yet. It's got you and me. His time will come, and I'm sure that when it does he'll be happy to take up his post here. But meanwhile he needs something more exciting. Let's hope this will be the answer.'

Louis was thrilled with the plan, and was all for setting off at once. The others insisted that the whole operation would have to be carefully planned. Angus got him to agree to this by stressing the element of risk.

'Spain's not a very safe country for foreigners at the moment. And for many Spaniards too, including Gil and Marta. If you do anything rash once you have contacted them it might have terrible repercussions. Remember, you will be the one link between them and their suspect past.'

'Harbouring a proven criminal like you, you mean?'

'Exactly. You'll be all right as long as you don't make any false moves.' Angus was having a difficult time, trying to make the enterprise seems as perilous as possible to Louis, and perfectly safe for Meg's benefit. 'But you've really got to do your homework. And the first thing is to learn Spanish.'

'Not Catalan?'

'No. That wouldn't go down at all well with the authorities. It has to be official Spanish. I can help you, but we'll have to get you a textbook, and you'll really have to work hard at it. And then we've still got to think of an excuse for your visit.'

'Could I be studying something?'

'Like what?'

'Flamenco dancing,' said Louis hopefully.

'Wrong part of Spain. Try again, seriously this time.'

'Well, what about geology? I could be studying the mountains on the southern slopes of the Pyrenees. How's that?'

'Excellent. How's your geology?'

'Never had any, I'm afraid.'

'Well then, you'd have a lot of hard work to do on that too.'

Louis didn't look very enthusiastic about this.

'I know!' Meg exclaimed. 'What about botany? That's something you do know a little about. Remember how we used to wander about looking at the wild flowers in the hedgerows? And then we always looked them up in the book when we got home.'

'Happiest days of my life.' Louis grinned.

Meg smiled indulgently.

'No, seriously,' went on Louis, 'I wouldn't at all mind mugging up some botany.'

So Louis started the serious study of Spanish and botany. His one protest was at the timescale. Angus insisted that he would have to wait till the late spring to set off.

'It'll take you that long to get to know the language well enough. And the botany. And besides, you can't go wandering about the Pyrenees till the winter's well and truly over. It's a fierce place, I can tell you.'

Louis accepted this limitation too, and got on with his studies. His imagination had been fired, and there was nothing he was not prepared to do to be able to make a success of the adventure. The thought of following his hero-father's footsteps appealed to him enormously. Also the idea that he could help to right what seemed to him such a terrible wrong. These people should at last know that the risks they had taken on behalf of his father had not been in vain.

As the time for Louis's departure approached, Angus spent many hours telling him as much as he could about where to head for. He had never been clear at the time as to where exactly he was. Since then he had looked for the village on the map, but it was evidently too small to be marked.

Once Louis found the village, things should be easier. Before leaving the *masia* Angus had got Gil to explain how far from the village it was, and in which direction it lay. He passed on this information to Louis and got him to memorize it. He stressed that he must not ask anyone about the whereabouts of the farm, but simply turn up as if he had come across it by chance in the midst of his botanical wanderings. Louis had also been made to promise that he would give up the whole idea if there were any hitches before finding Gil's house. They couldn't afford to be visited by any suspicious stranger.

One of the things that came under discussion with the whole family was the question of what Angus could send to his friends. It had to be something small and unobtrusive. They decided rosaries for Marta and Quimeta. Gil was more of a problem. At last Angus came up with the idea of binoculars. He remembered that Gil had once spoken to him about this wonderful invention that let you see distant things as if they were close to you. 'Every detail,' he said, 'every detail. *Una meravella.*'

Not long before his departure Louis announced that he intended to walk back over the Pyrenees, as his father had done.

'Well, I can't recommend the Devil's Gorge. I'd avoid that if I were you.'

'I don't suppose I could even find it. After all, you yourself had no idea where you were most of the time.'

Meg raised an objection:

'I think that sounds rather dangerous. Even avoiding the Devil's Gorge.'

'But this will be quite different. He won't be hiding from the authorities as I was. He'll be able to stick to the road if he wants. He'll be able to cross at any of the normal frontier posts.'

'Safe as houses,' said Louis reassuringly. 'And I could look up that old shepherd of yours when I'm at it.'

A few days later the family was gathered at the station again, waiting for the train to take Louis off on the first stage of his adventure. For different reasons they were all hoping it would be punctual – Louis because he couldn't wait to get started, the others because they wanted the parting over and done with. The train was late, and conversation flagged. Angus was afraid he hadn't been able to convey adequately to his son just how much he wanted to thank and bless Gil and Marta.

'Tell them . . . ' he began. And then he thought of Bob's abortive message to his parents. At that moment the train came in.

'I'll tell them,' said Louis confidently, 'I'll remember all you've told me.' As the train set off he leaned out of the window. Laughing, he took out the binoculars and focused them on his receding family.

That evening they all confessed that they felt a little bit flat, perhaps even sad.

'We'll certainly miss him,' said Meg.

Angus was just a little bit worried, though he didn't admit

this to the others. Along with this slight worry there was the satisfaction of knowing that Louis would perhaps go and see Alphonse.

'Well,' said Gavin, in one of the long silences that characterized that evening. 'The old have left us, and now the younger generation has gone too.'

'Yes,' said Angus, 'that just leaves us three middle-aged stick-in-the-muds.'

The other two burst out laughing.

'Hardly the *mot juste* for you,' said Meg.

'You may laugh,' said Angus, 'but I'm a reformed character now. You'll see.'

Gavin looked at his brother with an expression of indulgent scepticism. 'Time will show,' he said.

But Angus's thoughts had gone back to the expression he himself had just used. *Stick-in-the-mud*, he thought. The words seemed to be awakening an echo in the furthest corners of his mind. He couldn't quite think what it was, but felt sure it was of some significance. And then he remembered the story the shepherd had told about the stream calling the tree a stick-in-the-mud, just because it had roots and so stayed in the one place. Well, he thought, I've come back to my roots at last. Perhaps my wandering days are over now. Perhaps I can now play the part of the tree. Alphonse said that practically everything was possible in the real world.

Angus thought of his son setting out, like the stream, to see the world. And his thoughts were tinged with a touch of envy and a touch of apprehension – would Louis be all right? But beneath the envy and the apprehension there was a still, silent sense of peace and of homecoming. He could feel his roots at last. Perhaps the stream really could turn into a tree. Perhaps the shepherd was right.